The Masterpiece

RODNEY D. MOHR

authorHOUSE

AuthorHouse™
1663 Liberty Drive
Bloomington, IN 47403
www.authorhouse.com
Phone: 833-262-8899

*This is a work of fiction. All of the characters, names, incidents,
organizations, and dialogue in this novel are either the products
of the author's imagination or are used fictitiously.*

Published by AuthorHouse 10/26/2020

ISBN: 978-1-6655-0596-3 (sc)
ISBN: 978-1-6655-0595-6 (hc)
ISBN: 978-1-6655-0594-9 (e)

Library of Congress Control Number: 2020921122

Print information available on the last page.

This book is printed on acid-free paper.

To my father,
my mentor, my inspiration, and my friend.

Someone who could fix anything and
make something from nothing.

Most importantly, the one with
whom I shared my dyslexia.

Contents

Acknowledgments

As a dyslexic, I have struggled with the written word my entire life. Even though I have read a few books along the way, it has never been an enjoyable experience but more of an obstacle to conquer. I had an idea for a story that I had been thinking about for years, and when circumstances found me in a hotel room for two weeks at a time in Taiwan, it gave me the opportunity to try to write it down. Mostly, I saw it as an opportunity to work on my spelling and grammar, using it as something no one was ever going to read, but after I finished it, I showed it to some friends who thought it was worth trying to work into a longer version. After several years of effort, *The Masterpiece* was the result—but not without the help and encouragement from some special people.

Terry Carlin is a longtime friend and colleague who is as comfortable in the library as she is in her own home. Thank you so much for your encouragement, for listening to my ideas, and for giving me the feedback I needed to press on with my project.

Chris Germain read my very rough draft and made it clear to me the story was worth pursuing and cheered me on along the way.

My daughter, Kate, was an invaluable asset when it came to printing out each draft and, most importantly, listened to my many plot twists on our many hour-long trips in the car. Without your help, this book would never have come together.

Stacy Jerger made a guest blog on another editor's website that I happened to read when I was trying to figure out what to do with my first draft. She had described her business as a development editor, which sounded like the exact kind of help

I needed. After reading through my draft, she agreed to work with me to wrestle it into shape. What I gave her was a story with stick figures in a black-and-white world. By the time we were finished working together, my characters were fully formed and surrounded by a richly developed world. Without Stacy's help, there was no chance this story would have ever made it this far. Stacy, thank you so much for your help, and I cannot wait to work with you again.

Kevin Kelly made a comment one day as we walked home from work in Taiwan. "When you're done, let me read it, and if I like it, I'll give it to my sister-in-law who is an editor for Scribner." What a remarkable opportunity and a boost to my efforts to see it to completion. Kevin, I cannot thank you enough for even the possibility of having her read my story.

Because Kevin kept his word having read the book, he passed it on to Kathryn Belden, executive editor at Scribner, someone who I would have never thought would have taken the time to read my story past the first few pages. Kathryn, I can't tell you how meaningful your words were to me. Thank you for your encouragement!

Bruce Babbitt was one of the first people to read my story and has persistently encouraged me to get it published. Thank you, Bruce, for helping me push it over the finish line.

Most importantly, none of this would have happened without the help of my wife, Ann. You possessed an unceasing willingness to help me with every bit of the work that needed to be done. I know how difficult it is to deal with my dyslexia. Thank you for your perseverance and understanding. I love you with all my heart!

Chapter 1

❧❧❧

The Appraisal

"**C**AREFUL WITH IT!" PHIL SCOTT said as he and the delivery men steadied the mysterious bundle.

The lift gate on the delivery truck whined as it lowered. A tall object surrounded in shipping blankets secured with giant rubber bands was perched at its edge. The well-wrapped bundle disguised any hint of its contents, but Phil had a good feeling about it.

The wheels clattered as the delivery men rolled the dolly onto the loading dock and into the freight elevator. The doors opened on the seventh floor, and it was pushed into the storage room of Clement's Fine Art Auctions.

Later that afternoon, Phil Scott, Clement's American furniture expert, and his assistant, Sam, opened the door to the storage room and moved the still-wrapped bundle out into the sunlit showroom. Sam could handle the heavy lifting with ease, but to think he was all brawn and no brains would be a mistake. He was far prouder of his degree in fine art than of being a four-year letterman as a defensive end at Penn State. Phil, on the other hand, was a slender, refined man, ready for the cover of *GQ* magazine. He was pretty pleased with himself that he had hired Sam.

Unwrapping the bundle and closely examining the highboy, Sam remarked, "Phil, I think this is a really great piece. It has many of the elements of the Kirkman pieces we had two sales ago, but it looks a lot earlier."

"Let's take a look, shall we?" Phil said as they carefully removed the rest of the shipping blankets. He stood back to take in the magnificent highboy. "Sam, if we can get this right …"

"I know. I have a good idea what we have, but if we can put a name and a date on it, it's going to be big—really big. No doubt it's going on the cover of the catalog. We're looking at some seriously high bids if we can nail this as a Tabner Kirkman," Sam said as he became more excited at the possibilities.

"Okay, Sam! Let's not get ahead of ourselves. We have to get this right. Either we know it is or we're not sure, but there's no middle ground. Let's start with the big picture and then focus on the details."

"Yes, sir," Sam exclaimed as he grinned and got his notepad and pen ready.

"Okay … Connecticut dresser, likely from the 1850s or '60s, made with unbelievable American cherry with Queen Anne legs, claw-and-ball feet, carved fans, and three turned finials." After a slow stroll around the dresser, Phil stopped again at its front, placing a hand on his chin and silently mouthing *wow*.

They both stood back to appreciate it fully, not talking, just staring.

Finally, Phil said, "Time to look inside." He opened one of the drawers and looked at the dovetail joints. "There are three evenly spaced dovetails with the bottom two about one inch apart. That looks right. Go get the step stool, so I can get a closer look at the finials."

The highboy stood a full seven feet tall at the top of the crown. Sam slid the stool up to the side of the highboy, and Phil climbed up two steps. He stood at eye level with one of three unique finials. Its base looked like that of an old urn, and the top was carved in a slow spiral that resembled the flames of a torch.

He stepped down, slid the stool around to the front of the chest, and stepped back up to look at the top of the dresser. A fanlike shape was carved boldly in relief on the face of the small drawer. Phil drew his fingers across each groove of the fan as he considered the design. "I don't know about the shape of the fan. I've never seen this curl at the bottom. What do you think?"

Sam stepped onto the stool and studied it for a while. "I'm not sure.

Let me get my iPad, and I can pull up some pictures of the other pieces we've had."

After a few minutes, he returned with the device and located pictures from their archive with a few pokes at the screen. "See … Look right here—it's the same."

Phil climbed back on the stool, pulled out the top drawer, and looked at the fan again as Sam held up the iPad for simultaneous comparison. Finally, he nodded with approval and handed the drawer to his assistant. "Let's see what else is in here." As he looked back into the empty recess, he could see two finger holes. He reached inside and pulled out another drawer only about one and a half inches deep. "I think it's so cool that these old guys made these hidden drawers."

"Is there anything in it?" Sam asked inquisitively.

"Not this time." Phil slid the drawer back in place as Sam handed him the drawer with the carved fan. He pressed it slowly back in and was amazed how perfectly it fit. He stepped down off the stool and sat down next to Sam. They both stared at the highboy, studying every detail.

"You know, Sam, I've been looking at these things all my life and even grew up with something that looked a lot like this. It was in my dad's bedroom. I remember how thrilled he was when one day he removed a drawer that was sticking to put some wax on it so it would slide easier. When he turned it over, he found a big, beautiful, swirly signature that read *Sebastian Kirkman*. You could tell Sebastian was proud of it, and so was my dad. He got out his old Kodak camera and took a picture of it so he could show it off instead of taking his dresser apart. I think that was really what got me started."

As he finished his story, Phil looked over at Sam and saw that he was staring at the old dresser with a blank expression. "Sam?"

"Do you see what I'm seeing?!" Sam pointed at the figure in the wood moving across the drawers.

"Not sure. What?"

"I think I can see a landscape or waves of an ocean."

Still puzzled, Phil asked, "What are you talking about?"

Sam got up from his chair and pointed at the undulating lines made by the unusual figure in the wood. "Can you see the waves?"

Phil watched as Sam traced the shapes with his finger. He sat forward in his chair. "Oh my God! That's incredible! How did he do that? It's like he painted it with the figure in the wood. The design is perfect over the entire face of the dresser. I've never seen anything like it. And the drawer fronts are solid wood, not veneered."

Sam sat back down next to Phil and said in amazement, "How is it possible that no one knew about this piece for all these years? This has to be the best Kirkman piece ever to come up for auction!"

"My dad's old dresser was really close to this, but I think this is older. I think this really is *Tabner's work.* If we can prove this is old Tabner Kirkman's work, this is going to be huge!" Phil exclaimed. "Think of the publicity it could bring. I wonder if we are lucky enough to have some numbers." He stood and stepped behind the highboy, scanning the back with a small flashlight. After a few moments, he spotted a small set of numbers. "That's fantastic! We may be able to get a date and confirm it's made by Tabner Kirkman."

Phil went back to his office and thumbed through his stack of business cards until he found what he was looking for—the phone number of the one and only Benjamin Kirkman.

After a few rings, Benjamin's grandson picked up the phone. "Hello, Kirkman's. Tab speaking."

Benjamin laid his old Stanley plane on the workbench as he waited to see if it was for him.

After a moment, Tab replied, "Oh sure," and turned to Benjamin. "Hey, Grandpa, it's for you."

Benjamin brushed the sawdust from his calloused hands as he walked across the small, well-lit workshop, his old knees complaining as he sat on the stool in front of his drawing table. "Hello, can I help you?"

"Benjamin, it's so nice to hear your voice. It's Phil Scott from Clement's Fine Arts Auctions."

After they exchanged pleasantries, Phil said, "I think I have something for you to see. It's a highboy."

"Oh my, what a treat." Benjamin had known Phil since Phil was a little boy making visits with his father to the Kirkman's shop. He got a kick out of the little whiz kid with all his questions about the furniture in the workshop. Phil was about the same age as his own two sons, and Benjamin was thrilled to see him become the furniture expert for Clement's. Benjamin felt honored when Phil asked his opinion.

"We would love to have you come down and take a look at it. And, Benjamin, bring your book—we found some numbers."

"Numbers! Okay, now you've really piqued my interest."

They settled on a time to meet the following morning at the auction house.

Benjamin hung up the phone and turned to his grandson. Tradition was big in the Kirkman family, and Tab was named after old Tabner from generations ago. Like the Kirkmans before him, Tab had inherited a tall, slender build and wide grin.

"Well, Tab, we're going into the city. The auction house thinks they have a Kirkman highboy for their next sale. It's been a long time since I've seen an old highboy. We'll make a day of it."

"Sounds great, Grandpa!"

Tab had never seen a Kirkman highboy, and Benjamin was going to take full advantage of it. He took every opportunity to get his shy grandson out of the shop to meet people. This would be a good experience for him, and Tab would have a chance to meet someone who would be very interested in him.

"Let's call it a day and clean up. I'll see you at eight a.m. sharp to head into the city."

Tab took the bench brush and made a big pile of walnut chips to throw away. He littered dozens of chips while carving the claw-and-ball design onto the legs of a narrow hall table. He swept them into the trash can as his grandpa swept the floor.

The Kirkmans were well-known for their furniture. Their business was the oldest continuously operating furniture workshop in Connecticut. Benjamin had learned his craft from his father and grandfather before him, and now he was passing it on to his grandson, Tab. The two of them had worked together since Tab graduated from high school. Now, at the ripe old age of twenty-four, he was becoming an impressive craftsman.

At sixteen, Tab was left in Benjamin's care after his son, Charles, and daughter-in-law, Elizabeth, died. They had each other, but often Benjamin worried for his grandson and the future of the Kirkman workshop.

Tab's carving skills, sense of design, and eye for symmetry were impressive for a craftsman of his age. However, Benjamin knew Tab's heart wasn't in it, and he didn't show any interest in running the business. The day his parents died, a part of him died with them. He had lost his inner spark. Benjamin knew skill wasn't enough for success; it takes a real passion to thrive in this craft.

Benjamin often thought about what could have been—what great things could have been accomplished with his son, Charles, teaching Tab the trade. The three of them in the shop together would have been wonderful.

The next morning, they set off for New York City, Benjamin's old Ford Taurus plugging away. They parked in the underground garage around the corner from the auction house and entered the huge office building right on time. They headed up the elevator to the seventh floor. The elevator door opened right in front of the entrance to Clement's Fine Arts Auctions. Tab looked impressed with the stately gold leaf lettering on the glass of the door. He had never been there before, and Benjamin knew he wouldn't know what to expect.

Tab held the door as they entered. The receptionist had just finished giving someone a message. "May I help you?"

"Yes, I'm Benjamin Kirkman. We have an appointment with Phil Scott."

"Oh yes, one moment please." She reached down to buzz Phil's office.

After a few moments, Phil appeared from his office, greeting Benjamin with a big smile and a firm hand shake. "How are you, my friend? Thank you so much for coming in and helping us this morning. We think we have something special to show you."

"I want to introduce you to the next Kirkman craftsman, my grandson, Tabner. Tab has been working with me full time for several years now, and I think he really shows great promise."

Tab held out his hand and shyly said, "Pleased to meet you."

Benjamin watched Tab as he returned to his former stance, the one where he would stand with his hand behind his back grasping his other arm at the elbow. He could see Tab was uncomfortable with the praise and put his hand on Tab's shoulder. "I hope you can make it out to the shop some day and see some of Tab's fine work. I'm really pleased. He's a Kirkman through and through." Benjamin felt a great deal of pride in his young apprentice's progress.

"Tab, I'm pleased to meet you. If your grandfather says you're a promising craftsman, then I'm really looking forward to seeing your work."

Tab nodded in recognition of Phil's comments. Benjamin smiled and gave Tab's shoulder a squeeze.

Tab looked at him with that enough-is-enough look.

Benjamin knew he had limits on how far he could go before annoying his young apprentice. In many ways Tab was still the sixteen-year-old boy who came to live with him after his parents died.

"Can I get you anything? Water or a cup of coffee?" asked Phil as he motioned to each of them.

"I don't think I've ever turned down a cup of coffee," said Benjamin in anticipation.

"How about you, Tab? Would you like anything?" Phil asked.

Tab shook his head. "No, nothing for me, thank you."

As they walked past the office, they were met by Phil's assistant, Sam.

"Benjamin, I would like to introduce you to my new assistant, Sam. He has been working with me as an unpaid intern for the last few summers and now that he has graduated from college, we knew we wanted him full time. He has a great eye for furniture. He also found the highboy for the sale."

Benjamin smiled at the strapping young man as he held out his hand.

"Mr. Kirkman, it's an honor to meet you, sir. I can't tell you how much I admire your family's work." He vigorously shook Benjamin's hand.

"Now I'm beginning to blush," said Benjamin as he nudged Tab with his elbow.

Tab had a big grin on his face as he started to look a bit more comfortable. He reached out his hand and said, "Hi, I'm Tab."

"Tab, does that mean you're another Tabner?" asked Sam as he thought about the Kirkman's highboy.

He nodded and said, "Tabner Charles Kirkman."

"Okay, that's way cool! Anyway, I hate to meet and run, but I've got an appointment on Fifty-Seventh Street. It was great to meet you both," Sam said as he hurried out the door.

Just as Sam left, Sandy appeared with Benjamin's coffee. By now his attention was split by the pleasantries and the highboy he could see in the distant adjacent room.

Benjamin could hardly stand it, "Thank you for the coffee." He looked at Phil and pointed toward the awaiting highboy, "Can we?"

Phil said, "Oh, sure," as he motioned them into the auction room where the highboy was waiting.

Benjamin's eyes lit up as if he were seeing a long-lost friend. He stood at a distance just taking it in. He recognized every line and curve; nothing was unfamiliar even though he was seeing this highboy for the first time.

After a moment, Benjamin stepped forward to get a closer look. He grinned as he ran his hand across the now rippled figure of the richly colored cherry.

Tab followed him around, trying to see what Benjamin was seeing. Benjamin pointed out details for Tab as his hand led him around the highboy.

"Could I use something to get a closer look at the crown?" Even though Benjamin was six three, the dresser was still over his head.

"Oh, of course." Phil had the stool ready in anticipation. "Here you are," he said as he set it down in front of the highboy.

Benjamin scooted it a little to the right and stepped up until he was eye level with the finial. He looked at it for a while and then caressed the fiery flutes with his fingertips, marveling at the detailed craftsmanship. He was impressed with how cleanly every cut had been made. He could see lots of toolmarks, but they didn't seem to take anything away from the charm. In fact, he thought they added to the look. He thought even the slightest bit of sanding would have taken away the crispness and bold character of the carving.

Then he focused his attention on the top drawer with the carved fan. His fingers moved along the bottom detail of the fan, feeling how it curled around. *Was there an extra line, almost like a shadow?* he thought.

He pulled out the drawer and looked at the dovetail layout, three even and the last two an inch apart.

"Here, Tab. Take this," Benjamin said as he handed him the drawer.

Tab took the drawer from him, sat in a chair, and took a turn looking over the fan carving.

Benjamin reached in and pulled out the little drawer and handed it to Tab.

Tab chuckled and said, "What's this?"

Benjamin said, "The nineteenth-century idea of a home safe."

"You're kidding, right?" Tab chuckled again as he looked it over.

"No, the gentleman of the house needed some place to hide his valuables from uninvited guests—and even some who were invited."

Benjamin pulled a small flashlight out of his pocket, shined it into the open space, and looked deep inside. He could see a faintly drawn *X* with a little hole drilled in the center at the back of the opening. He could see the hiding place for the blessing, a Kirkman tradition that Benjamin continued.

He pulled his flashlight back and mumbled under his breath, "That's where I would have put it."

Tab said, "What was that, Grandpa?"

"Oh, nothing. Hand those things up here, and I'll put them back." Benjamin slid the drawers back into place and stepped off the step stool a little off balance.

"Oh, careful, Benjamin," Phil said, reaching toward him in case he fell.

"It's these old knees. My doctor says I need new ones, but I'm kind of partial to the originals."

Benjamin straightened up and walked around to the left side of the highboy for a closer look. There was little doubt in his mind who had made the highboy. The unique fan design, the swirled flame finials, and the way the claws were carved on the long Queen Anne legs—all the little details were easy for Benjamin to read. This was a highboy by Tabner Kirkman.

Now it was time to find the numbers and check them against his little book. He ran his hand across the back and down to the joint between the upper and lower cabinet. He felt them faintly scratched into the wood. "Here they are."

"How did you know where they were?" asked Tab.

"I had a hunch. They could be on the other side too, but I'm pretty sure this is old Tabner's work. If it were Floyd, Tabner's father, it would have been on the other side."

"Why on the other side?"

"Because he was left-handed," Benjamin said with a grin.

Benjamin looked down at the numbers and copied them down and then straightened up and walked over to the window. He took a small, tattered book out of his jacket pocket and started thumbing through the pages.

Tab walked over to the highboy and stood next to it. Just as Benjamin did, he bent over to find the numbers. He slid his hand over the old pine back until he found four small numbers. "Five, six, one, one," he said out loud. "Hey, Grandpa, why are they upside down?"

He replied back, "Think about it."

Tab walked around the back to get a better look. He knelt down and put his hand up as if to scratch them in himself, popped back up, went back to the side of the highboy and bent over to look at the numbers again.

After a moment he said, "Okay, I get it. That's where he stood, and he bent over to scratch the numbers in, and of course his father's would be on the other side. Duh."

Benjamin said, "You got it."

He continued to look through the book, page after page. The numbers didn't always make a lot of sense because they were not sequential, and different members of the family had different numbering systems. Benjamin figured the numbers had to be old Tabner's and that the piece was early in his career—really early.

When he found a page that had the five, six numbers, his heart raced with a sense of excitement and discovery. He slid his finger up the page to 5611. On that line, it said in tiny letters: "highboy cherry Thomas Bellingham, Hartford." Because there wasn't any more room on that line, there were two more words along the margin: "my first."

Benjamin dropped his hands down to his sides, stood in front of the highboy, and stared at it again. He could hardly believe what he was seeing. This was it—the legendary Tabner Kirkman highboy he had heard so much about since he was a little boy.

After Old Tabner had made this dresser, he spent the rest of his working life making furniture for the Hartford elite. This was the piece that had changed everything for the Kirkman's shop.

It was an emotional moment for Benjamin. He spent his entire career aspiring to equal the work of old Tabner. Now he was spending his last days in the shop teaching his namesake.

"Well, gentlemen, you're looking at a cherry highboy made by Tabner Kirkman in 1856 for Thomas Bellingham of Hartford. He made hundreds and hundreds of pieces of furniture of all different kinds."

He turned to his grandson with pride and shared some history. "Tab, this was his very first piece as elder craftsman. This is *really* something special."

Benjamin looked at Phil and said with a big grin, "You've really got something this time."

"This is fantastic! We have several clients who are Kirkman collectors. I'm looking forward to inviting them in for a private viewing of the first Tabner Kirkman. Thank you so much for coming in. You've really made my day!"

"Phil, this has been a real treat. Thanks so much for asking us to come in. It was great seeing something so special."

"I'll send you a catalog as soon as they are ready, and of course you are invited to the reception the night before the sale."

He shook Benjamin's hand and then Tab's. "Tab, it was very nice to meet you. Maybe someday we'll be selling one of your masterpieces."

Tab reached out and shook his hand and said, "It's going to be a long time before I make something as beautiful as that."

"Well, not if you stick with your grandfather. He'll make you into a master craftsman in no time."

As Phil walked them out, he said, "Tab, I want to give you something." He opened a door behind the receptionist's desk and began to rifle through the many glossy catalogs. He selected a few and set them on the counter. "There should be one more … Ah, here it is."

He straightened up the stack of about five catalogs and handed them to Tab. "Take these home with you. There are a lot of fantastic pieces of furniture in these. They should be a great source of inspiration. Believe it or not, there's a Kirkman piece in every one of them."

Tab thanked him for his generosity. Benjamin gave Phil a grateful smile.

Tab fumbled with the catalogs as he reached for the elevator button to get to the lobby.

"You've got quite a haul," said his grandfather, wishing he could help.

"Yeah, that was really nice of him to give me so many."

"I think you will enjoy going through them. I'm sure there are some nice pieces in them. They have very nice things in their sales, and it will be very beneficial to see the old pieces and their values."

They made their way out of the building and to the parking lot. Looking a little tired, the sun-faded Taurus was waiting for them.

As if reading his thoughts, Tab said, "Hey, Grandpa, when are you going to get rid of this old thing?"

"I drove my last Ford more than four hundred thousand miles, and this car is going to go at least that far. Why should I spend so much money on a new car when this one runs like a top? Besides, if I find myself in a situation where I need to drive around in a new car, I can always borrow yours, right?"

"The thought of you driving down the road in my silver Mustang with the windows down wearing your blue Dickies work shirt, and your white hair wafting in the breeze makes me laugh every time I think about it." Tab added, "I think all your car needs is a fresh coat of wax, and it'll look twenty years younger."

"You know, Tab, I think you're right. Why don't you stay after work tomorrow, and we'll give it a good shine."

"Okay, I guess I walked straight into that one."

Benjamin turned his car north as they headed out of the city on their two-and-a-half-hour trip back to Hartford. As they crossed into Connecticut, they began talking about the highboy. Benjamin asked his young apprentice what he thought about his namesake's work.

"I was surprised to see it was in such good condition. There were only a few scratches and chipped corners. Whoever owned it for all these years took very good care of it."

Benjamin agreed but wanted him to look deeper than just the condition. "How did it make you feel when you first saw it?"

Tab stared straight ahead, seeming to be deep in thought. "I didn't feel anything."

"Really? You didn't feel anything? It didn't evoke any feelings at all?"

Tab looked at him like he'd said something wrong.

"Come on, Tab, think. How did it make you feel? Close your eyes, and see it in your mind's eye."

Tab sat there for a while, keeping his eyes closed. Finally, he said, "Warm ... It gave me a warm feeling."

Benjamin kept looking straight ahead. "What do you mean, *warm*?"

"I've never thought about how a piece of furniture makes me feel. It's just a thing. But now, as I think about it, there's something about it that makes me want to look at it and really study it. Am I right?"

"Okay, you're definitely on the right track. Now tell me what you saw."

Tab sat back in his seat and sighed loudly with relief.

"Well ... First of all, it's a very showy piece with its thin, curvy legs. And the way he laid out the wood was important to the look. The figure in the wood made it look like it was a chestnut-colored piece of marble. It was crazy how he made the pattern in the wood match all the way up to the top drawer."

Benjamin could see Tab getting more animated as he went on about the highboy.

"The three turned finials were very cool, with the turned lower part and the carved upper. You know, I had a different feeling about it when I was standing in front of it than when I was standing on the stool." Tab shifted himself a bit in his seat to better look at him.

Benjamin liked what he was hearing. "Did you like the finials better up close or from the floor?"

Tab brushed his hair out of his eyes as he answered. "Well, both. From the ground they looked bold and crisp, but up close they were full of toolmarks that I didn't notice from below. They didn't seem to take anything away from the look; in fact, I think they looked cool."

"Cool ... What do you mean, *cool*?"

"Well, it made them kind of bold—kind of in your face."

"In your face?"

"Yeah, you know … here I am! Kind of rough and ready."

Benjamin grinned and said, "Why do you think he left them with all those toolmarks on such a refined piece?"

"I don't know. I couldn't see how rough they were until I was right up close to them."

Benjamin said, "That's exactly right. You can't see it from so far away, so why not leave them like that? If you sanded the toolmarks away, you would lose some of the crispness that makes them look so good from the floor. So, what did you think about the fans carved in the drawers?"

"It was very cool that they were the opposite of each other."

Benjamin took his eyes off the road to look over at Tab. "What do you mean, *opposite*?"

"They were mirror images of each other in every detail. The fan on the bottom was cut deep into the drawer face, and the one on the top drawer stood out from the face as far as the other was deep."

"Tab, why do you think he made them that way?"

They drove a few miles down the road before Tab took a stab at the answer. "They balance each other out, like yin and yang, but maybe it was just showing off."

Benjamin said, "I think you're right. It's the balance of the design and maybe a little showing off too. The whole thing is showing off. It's the craftsman showing off his wood carving skills—his ability to have the most beautiful wood and knowing how to use it to his best advantage. And maybe, most importantly, it's the new owner's status of having something so beautiful and expensive."

"You know, I was thinking about this at the auction house when the light was shining on that wonderful, rich color and the fantastic patina of the old antique. Somehow, it almost gave it a lifelike character. Every dent, scratch, and worn bit of finish was a testament to its 160-plus years of life."

Benjamin was pleased that the experience of seeing the old treasure would have such a profound impact on him. The Kirkmans were famous for the high quality of their work. It made their furniture highly collectable. However, he wanted Tab to see more than just the shape of the piece. He wanted him to have an emotional experience when he looked at old family pieces.

Tab's enthusiasm for furniture didn't seem to be a passion yet, and Benjamin knew that it had to be for him to make furniture the Kirkman way.

Benjamin's knees began to throb with a dull pain. He was feeling every one of his seventy-five years, from his bad knees to the twinge he felt every morning from his arthritic hands. Every day it became clear to him that if the Kirkman shop was going to continue, Tab would have to take on the major part of the work soon. Would he be ready?

Benjamin's time to help Tab learn the craft was limited, and it was time to give his apprentice a big challenge.

Chapter 2

❧ ❧

The Auction

"MR. KING, PHIL SCOTT FROM Clement's calling. I think I have something you're going to want to see—a very fine Tabner Kirkman highboy. It's the best we've ever had, and it's really early."

"Tell me more. How early?" Mr. King was one of many Kirkman collectors.

"We have confirmation from one of Tabner Kirkman's living relatives, a great-great-great-grandson by the name of Benjamin Kirkman. He came in last week to evaluate it."

"You've definitely piqued my interest. Can you email me some pictures?"

"I already have. They should be in your email now."

"Give me a moment."

"While you're looking, I would like to invite you down for a private viewing."

"Okay ... Here they are. Wow, that's a handsome piece! Let me call my wife, and I'll get right back with you. I'm sure she would love to join me."

Phil made at least a dozen more calls that morning to invite all his Kirkman collectors for a private look. Most were anxious to take a look.

Mr. Campbell called back and insisted on an appointment at Phil's earliest convenience. "Phil, I'm just a few hours from getting on a plane, and I'll be out of town for the better part of the week. My schedule is still pretty full once I return, and our golf charity event is next week, remember?"

"Well, if you can make it in, we'll have it here waiting for you to take a look."

"Thanks, Phil. I'll hop in a cab, and I'll see you in a few minutes."

"That's great! See you in a few minutes."

Phil felt a wave of panic come over him as he jumped out of his chair and threw off his jacket, neatly placing it over his chair. He wasn't used to moving this fast, ever, but he wanted to be ready.

He barked out to the receptionist. "Sandy, call Sam and tell him to meet me on the auction floor, and when you're done, come out and help me move some of the chairs out of the way."

Phil wanted to put the highboy in the middle of the auction room where the morning sun would highlight its best features so Mr. Campbell could see it glow.

Sam entered the room at a trot and said, "What do you need?"

"The Kirkman, front and center."

"Whoa! We've got next week's auction right in front of it."

Phil ran his hands through his hair as the stress of the moment turned his face hot and agitated. Clement's Manhattan location was packed into a few small offices. The storage room was a long narrow room, forcing all the departments to share the same cramped space.

"You have ten minutes to get it out here." Phil barked as he continued to stack chairs and push them to the far wall. Phil was out of breath. With one hand on his hip, he pulled out his crisp white handkerchief and wiped his brow. He looked a bit miffed at Sam's inaction.

Seeing his boss's irritation, Sam flung open the double doors of the storage room. It was packed with all the decorative arts items that would be up for auction this weekend. Many of the items were on tables still in plastic tubs. The highboy was barely visible at the back of the room. "You've got to be kidding!"

Phil looked at him with a real sense of urgency, "We have to get it out there," he said, pointing to the showroom.

"We can't move all these things without risking some kind of disaster. There's only one way to get it out of there, and that's through the lobby!"

"What?!" exclaimed Phil.

"We can put it in the freight elevator from the back of the storage room, then on to the loading dock, down the alley, around to the front of the building, and up the front elevator."

Phil looked at him in disbelief. "You've got to be out of your mind!"

Sam said with certainty, "I think we've got about six minutes left. Your call." He rolled up his sleeves in anticipation of the physical challenge; either way, his boss was going to go full steam ahead. He wasn't one to shy away from a challenge. Sam was rock solid, having spent nearly every weekend in some kind of sport since he was five years old.

Phil put his hand on his forehead and grit his teeth. "Okay, let's go. I must be out of my mind," he said, shaking his head in disbelief.

Sam slapped his hands together as if the quarterback had just called the play. He banged the freight elevator call button with an open hand.

"Come on, come on … This dumb thing is so slow."

Sam smiled at Phil. "You'd better roll up your sleeves. This is going to take everything we have to get this done."

The elevator finally clicked into place.

"This better work, Sam!" Phil removed his cufflinks and started to turn over the cuffs of his well-starched shirt sleeve.

Sam threw up the gate, and Phil helped him roll the highboy on to the elevator and slammed the gate shut behind them.

"It will. I know it will. I've done it before."

"You've done it before? Are you serious?"

"You guys are always asking me to do the impossible."

The elevator thumped and jerked as it came to a stop on the first floor. Sam lifted the freight elevator gate and unlocked the freight door. They pushed the highboy onto the loading dock and over to the ramp. Phil looked at Sam and emphatically said, "No way. You've got to be kidding!"

"Don't worry. We can do this." Sam moved around to the side and prepared to lower it down the slope. "Come on. Come over here and help me lower it down … Easy, easy, okay, we've got it."

They both breathed a sigh of relief. Now they had to push it through the alley and all the way around to the front of the building, through the front door, into the elevator, up to the seventh floor, and into the showroom.

A nervous wreck, Phil looked down at his watch and said, "We've only got three minutes."

Phil and Sam pushed the highboy around to the street with its dolly wheels clattering all the way.

The two men received quite a few strange looks as they pushed it through the front door, into the lobby, and then up to the elevator door.

Heaving a sigh of relief, Phil looked at Sam and breathlessly said, "Home free."

The elevator door opened, and they started to push it in, but the public elevator was much smaller than the freight elevator.

Suddenly, Sam yelled, "Stop! It's too tall!"

The seven-foot-tall beauty was six inches too tall to fit through the elevator door.

Phil yelled, "Back it up. We'll have to take it off the dolly and tip it in headfirst." They wrestled it into place as Phil grunted under the strain.

Concerned that Phil might have hurt himself, Sam asked, "Are you okay?"

Phil stood up, rubbed his lower back and wiped his forehead with the sleeve of his starched shirt before he realized what he was doing. He shook his head and said, "I'm glad I don't do this kind of thing every day." He pulled his crumpled handkerchief from his pocket again. "Sam, it looks like there's only room for one of us. You'll have to take the stairs."

Phil hit the button for the seventh floor and leaned back as the elevator doors closed. The bell dinged as the elevator lurched to a stop. As the doors opened, Sandy was ready to help by holding the doors open. When the elevator doors opened, she saw the highboy and yelled back into the auction house for more help. Three more employees briskly approached from around the corner.

"Come on. Help me with this thing," grunted Phil.

With a few grunts and groans, they had it out of the elevator and back on to the dolly headed toward the showroom.

Just then, Sam entered the showroom huffing and puffing from his sprint up seven flights of stairs. After the highboy was placed in just the right spot, Phil hurried back to his office to freshen up. He always kept a fresh shirt in his closet just in case he spilled something at lunch.

He was checking himself in the mirror as he slipped his jacket on just in time to hear the receptionist's buzzer.

"Mr. Scott, your client is here."

"Thank you, Sandy. I'll be right out." He took another quick glance in the mirror, tugging his tie to the center. Still trying to catch his breath, he paused for a moment, his hand on the doorknob. He stepped into the lobby just in time to greet Mr. Campbell.

"Mr. Campbell, it's so nice to see you. Thank you for coming. I think we've got something very special."

"Let's take a look. I have to leave for the airport soon."

Phil motioned the way toward the showroom. As they entered, Mr. Campbell got his first glimpse of the piece. The old dresser stood in the middle of the room as the midday sun bathed its richly colored and figured cherry. He stood next to Phil, taking a moment to look it over.

"Okay, Phil, tell me about it," Mr. Campbell finally said.

"We are very pleased to offer this highboy made in the Chippendale style with its highly figured cherry and white pine secondary wood, which was common for Connecticut makers. We now know that it is the work of Tabner Kirkman."

Mr. Campbell continued to look over the dresser as he listened. "Phil, this is beautiful, but how do we know it's Tabner Kirkman's work?"

Phil had done business with Mr. Campbell for years and knew he was a very careful collector. He knew that if he couldn't back up his statements with facts, Mr. Campbell wasn't going to place a bid.

"Okay, first, we have the carved fans that are consistent with other confirmed Tabner pieces." Phil walked over and pulled open one of the drawers and pointed to the dovetails. "Second, he always made them with three evenly spaced dovetails and two one inch apart. Third, the finials are carved like flames. These three things are pretty definitive, but we have more. There are numbers on the back."

"How does that help you?"

"Benjamin Kirkman has an old ledger that matches up with the numbers, so we also have a date: 1856."

"Will it be sold with any of this documentation?"

"I will make arrangements to have a document written. But wait, there's more."

"More?"

Phil walked over to Mr. Campbell and said with a grin, "In the margin of the ledger is a note in Tabner's hand writing that says this is his first piece as the elder craftsman."

Mr. Campbell stood back and covered his mouth with his hand. "It's his first?"

"Yes, sir."

"And you can get that documented too?"

"I will talk to Mr. Kirkman and see what we can do."

Mr. Campbell stared in silence for a while just to take it all in. After a few moments, he spoke. "How about provenance?"

"Unfortunately, we don't have much. It was bought at a consignment sale about thirty years ago. Before that, nothing, but the ledger also gives us the name of the first owner: Thomas Bellingham of Hartford."

"Well, that's something. Have you done any research on him?"

"My assistant Sam has found a little. He was in the insurance business, mostly insuring shipping."

Mr. Campbell looked delighted and seemed to want to say more, but he glanced at his watch.

"Oh, I've got to get going, or I'll miss my plane." He reached for his bag and coat and headed for the door. Before stepping into the elevator, he turned and shouted, "I'll see you at the sale! Get those documents, and thanks for the call." In a flash, he was gone.

Phil plopped himself down in a chair. He was still overheated from the moving ordeal.

He began taking his jacket off just as Sam entered back into the room.

"I hope that was worth the effort," said Sam.

"Mr. Campbell never tips his hand, but there's no doubt that he's a bidder. All I had to say was 'Tabner's first,' and I knew we had him. I can't believe we pulled that off. Sam, you earned your pay for the day. I'll even treat you to lunch." He stood up and started toward his office.

"We'll go after you put it back. We've got a sale to set up tomorrow, you know."

Sam fell into the chair exhausted. "I'm not sure I have an appetite anymore!"

Tab struck the oak wedge with three hard blows using a wooden mallet. This permanently fixed the chair legs into the seat. He was doing the final assembly on the new Windsor back chair after several trial fits.

He set the chair upright on the table and looked at each side to make sure everything was aligned properly. After a few tweaks, he twisted and tugged it into shape, making sure it stood on all four feet.

He ignored the ringing phone until he was satisfied it was perfect. Knowing dried glue was unforgiving, any distraction could spell disaster.

He picked up the phone in his grandfather's office as he wiped the leftover glue off the chair leg. "Hello, Kirkman's."

"Well, hello. Is this Tab?"

Tab recognized the voice. "Yes, Mr. Scott. I wanted to thank you again for the catalogs. I looked through every one several times. It was great to see the old Kirkman pieces too."

"Tab, I'm glad you got so much out of the catalogs. Hang on to them. They can be a good reference for the future."

"I'm looking forward to seeing the next one. Anyway, if you're calling for my grandfather, he's down in the woodshed cutting out parts for our next project."

"I need to ask him a favor Tab. Is now a good time, or shall I call back later?"

"Let me run down to the shed and get him."

Tab could hear the whir of the table saw as he trotted down and around the side of the old shop. The saw shop had been added to the business back in the 1940s when his grandfather was just a boy.

Tab entered the saw shop and waited for his grandfather to finish what he was cutting before he got his attention. Tab put his hand up to his ear as if it were a phone.

His grandfather reached down and shut off the table saw, brushed the sawdust off his shirt, and took out his earplugs.

Tab shouted out, "Phil Scott," over the still running dust collector.

His grandfather nodded and walked back to the workshop with Tab. He reached for the phone and sat down at his desk. "Kirkman's," he said with a loud voice.

Tab lingered nearby, curious what the call was about.

"Oh, hi, Phil. Well, my ears are ringing from the table saw, but other than that, I'm well. What can I do for you? … That's great, Phil. I'm glad to hear the highboy has gotten so much interest."

Tab's excitement increased too. The more Tab thought about the highboy, the more he thought about having a chance to look it over again. Tab didn't realize the value of it until he saw there were similar pieces in the catalogs, including one from Philadelphia with a sales estimate that was more than $100,000. He was anxious to see what the estimate would be for old Tabner's highboy.

His grandfather periodically nodded as Phil continued to speak.

"Phil, I'll be happy to write you the letter that it's Tabner's first piece, but I can't let the ledger be copied. I know I can trust you, but I don't want it to be used to number some fake old pieces so someone can make a few bucks. I'm sorry. I'll tell you what I am willing to do. I'll allow you to display it in one of your cases with your assurance that there will be no photos." There was a pause, and then Tab heard, "Thanks, Phil, for your understanding."

Tab shifted in the doorway, his grandfather glancing at him with a smile. Tab knew that smile. His grandfather was up to something.

"The day before and the day of … We can do that. Tab wanted to go to the reception anyway."

After a few more moments, his grandfather hung up the phone and looked over at him.

"I never said I wanted to go to any reception," he said, tensing at the thought of schmoozing with crowds of fancy strangers. He struggled for the right excuse. "Anyway, it's way too much driving to drive back the next day for the auction."

"Phil has graciously offered a hotel room for the two of us for the evening of the reception."

"I can't sleep in the same room with you. You shake the plaster off the walls when you snore. I'll have to sleep in the car," said Tab with a grin.

"I'm pretty sure he said *suite*. That means you'll have your own room."

"I think I'd rather skip the reception and drive up the day of the auction."

"Oh, come on, Tab. You'll have a great time. Maybe you'll meet a nice young lady."

"Thanks, Grandpa, but I don't need any help in the lady department." Tab wasn't interested in the girls he'd met. He had connected with only one girl in his life; however, she was currently halfway across the world.

"Really? When was the last time you were on a date?"

"A couple of months ago."

"A couple of months ago? I think you've lost your ability to tell time. It was almost a year ago."

When was the last time he was on a date? Tab thought to himself. Besides, he hated going on dates.

"Okay, it was a year ago, whatever. Anyway, if they have enough money to buy anything at that auction, they are way out of my league."

"All right, I'll stop trying to play matchmaker, but I think it's important for you to go and get some experience introducing yourself to your potential customers."

"Okay! I'll go, but just business. No matchmaking. Just behave yourself!"

"I promise."

While his grandfather scribbled a few notes on the back of an old envelope, Tab pondered his grandfather's words. He knew his grandfather was right. He should go and meet new people and be social. After his parents died, most of his classmates and friends didn't know how to interact with him. They just kept their distance like he had some kind of an illness they didn't dare catch. He really didn't spend any time with any of them anyway.

He had only a few friends he wanted to be with, if only they hadn't moved away.

Willy, his best friend since kindergarten, and Willy's wife, Celeste, moved away and had two kids. Then there was Isabella, Celeste's twin sister. The four of them were quite a group in high school, but that felt like ages ago.

It had been years since Isabella moved across the globe. She hadn't sent a letter in months. What was she doing? Was she ever coming back?

Other than his grandfather, no one could make Tab feel complete except Isabella. They helped each other through rough times. They were best friends, the kind you never forget, your rock-in-a-storm kind of friend. He just wanted Isabella to come home.

Tab had a tough time with loss. He had convinced himself long ago that if he didn't make new friends or go on dates with girls, he wouldn't feel bad when he lost them.

His grandfather's voice interrupted his thoughts. "I'm heading in the house to write Phil's letter. I hope I have some carbon paper. I want to have a copy for myself."

"What's the carbon paper for?"

"How else would you make a copy when you type up a letter?"

"Just push print!"

"There's no print key on my typewriter."

"Holy cow, does everything you do have to be the way they did it in the nineteenth century?"

"It's worked just fine for whatever I've been asked to do."

"Wow! We have to get you into the twenty-first century."

"Well, I do drive a car," Benjamin said with a cocky voice.

"Yeah, but that car isn't even from the twenty-first century. It's almost as old as I am."

His grandfather just laughed and headed into the house. Tab frowned at his grandfather's slow gait, knowing his old knees were complaining all the way.

A couple of days later, Tab walked into the shop with the mail.

"Hey, Grandpa, you're going to love this." He handed the mail over to his grandfather with a big grin.

His grandfather thumbed through the mail until he came across a large envelope from Clement's Fine Arts Auctions, "Hey, it's already open."

"Yeah, I know. I couldn't wait."

His grandfather reached into the envelope and pulled out a large glossy catalog. He held it up to the light to get a good look at the cover. "Well, look at that. Isn't that something?"

Tab was overly excited and proud. "Old Tabner made the cover. What do you think of that?"

His grandfather ran his fingers over the picture of the highboy as if he were caressing the old dresser itself. "It looks as good on the cover as it looks in real life. Won't it be exciting to watch it sell?"

Tab nodded. "Can you believe it? It could sell for $100,000. I hope we get a chance to meet the new owner."

The two weeks between the arrival of the catalog and the auction passed by in a flash. Tab had mixed emotions about the reception. He was interested in seeing who would come to look at the highboy, but he loathed the thought of his grandfather bragging about his work or wanting him to meet every single woman in the room.

The big day started early with the drive into New York City. Tab could tell his grandfather was really looking forward to the day at the auction house and talking to potential buyers and admirers of old Tabner's work.

He'd said on more than one occasion that he was deeply honored to be a part of nearly two centuries of Kirkman craftsmen.

For the first time in his life, Tab started to get it. For his grandfather, it wasn't a job that he went to every day; it was something that he loved and felt truly blessed to have done all his life.

Tab watched with delight as his grandfather strutted into the Clement's building and onto the elevator, seemingly ignoring his creaky old knees for the first time in a while.

His grandfather looked at him and said, "This is going to be an interesting and, I think, fun day."

Tab nodded as the elevator stopped with a few short jerks. He agreed; this *was* going to be an interesting day. He had never attended anything like this before.

Clement's appeared to be a busy place. Sandy smiled from behind the reception desk. "Good morning, Mr. Kirkman, Tab. How are you both this morning? Phil is on the sixth floor; he will be up in a few minutes."

She pointed at his grandfather and said, "I know you want coffee." Then she pointed at Tab. "Do you want anything?"

Tab nodded. "Sure, I would love some coffee."

Phil hustled into the room wearing a big smile. He reached out to shake both of their hands. "Thank you so much for coming. We've had so much interest in the highboy since the catalog was sent. I think it's going to be an eventful day."

Phil motioned them toward the showroom and then led them to an empty case. "Benjamin, this is where the ledger will be displayed. We'll have someone with it at all times, and I assure you that there will be no photos. We're used to people trying to sneak shots with their cell phones, so we'll keep a close eye on it."

"I understand, Phil. I'm sure your staff will do their best."

His grandfather took the ledger out of his pocket, opened it to the right page, and handed it over like it was the crown jewels.

Phil took the ledger with equal reverence and placed it on top of a stand in the middle of the case that held it close to the glass so the inscription could be easily read. "What do you think?"

"It looks good," Benjamin replied assuredly.

"We really appreciate your assistance. Several of our clients are looking forward to meeting you as well. Most of them had no idea there were any Kirkmans still working."

His grandfather glanced sideways at Tab with a twinkle in his eyes.

Phil took his keys out of his pocket and locked the case. "All right, I think we're ready."

Throughout the morning, a steady stream of people visited Clement's to view the three hundred plus items to be offered at the auction the following day.

Tab walked around looking at each of the items and reading the descriptions in the catalog. Only a small number of items had photos in the catalog.

After a while, Tab began to understand how items were arranged for the sale. There was a rise and fall of prices that went in several cycles throughout the auction.

Several pieces toward the middle of the auction had the highest estimates. The Tabner highboy was the finale, but it didn't have the highest estimate.

Tab was a bit confused about why they arranged the auction this way.

During the viewing, there was a rare moment when Phil was not with an auction patron. Tab approached him and asked him about why he had arranged the items the way he did.

"We try to mix the lower-priced items with the more expensive items for one important reason. We want to keep buyers in their seats ready to buy. We have several higher-priced items dispersed throughout the auction, which keeps things interesting. However, we always try to save the best for last."

"Why is the highboy the best? It isn't the highest priced piece in the sale."

"Oh, but it's by far the most interesting, and don't be surprised if it isn't the highest priced sale of the day."

"You really think it will be?" Tab said in disbelief.

"Well, we have some patrons who have left bids that are going to surprise you."

All this felt so strange. He had been around the shop all his life and had seen his grandfather make some amazing things. Old Tabner's dresser was something different, bathed in a century and a half of age. It had a personality all its own.

Tab watched as auction patrons marveled at its beauty. It all felt surreal to Tab, knowing it came from his family. What were they thinking? Was it really as nice as his grandfather thought it was? Some patrons lingered longer than others. Most of them couldn't help touching the decorative fans and the rippled texture of the old cherry.

His grandfather enjoyed the afternoon meeting and talking to so many people who were admiring his family's work. It didn't take long before Tab began to enjoy himself too. Some of them even expressed interest in seeing the furniture the two of them were building.

It was nearly five o'clock that evening when his grandfather said, "I've got to go to the hotel and get off these old feet."

Tab jumped into caregiver mode and helped his grandfather head for their hotel. "Let's take a cab, it'll save you a few steps."

It was only a two-minute ride, but Tab felt it was worth every penny.

He was concerned his grandfather had overdone it as he watched him rub his knees.

"Grandpa, are you okay?"

"Oh, sure, but the old knees sure need a rest."

The clerk at the desk had told them earlier that they would have their bags delivered to the room by early evening.

After picking up the room keys, Tab held his grandfather's arm, something he hadn't done since he was a little boy. He helped him into the elevator and up to the room.

"Wow! Look at this place! I've only seen something like this in the movies." The suite was nearly twice the size of Tab's apartment. There were two bedrooms, each with its own bathroom covered in white marble.

"Tab, we're living in luxury tonight."

"Hey, Grandpa, look at this … They gave us a nice platter with some fruit and cheese, and there's a card."

Tab opened the letter and read it out loud.

> *Welcome to the Branford. Please accept this gift and enjoy your stay.*
>
> *William Falstaff, General Manager*

"They sure know how to make you feel special, don't they, Tab? I think I'm going to lie down for a while. Please don't let me sleep past six thirty. I don't want to miss the reception tonight. Phil said there was someone that he wanted to introduce us to."

"Okay, Grandpa. I'll just hang out in my room and watch some TV."

His grandfather propped himself up in his bed with all four pillows, and within a few minutes, he was fast asleep. Tab watched his grandfather snore from his open door.

For so long, his grandfather seemed to never age, but seeing him fast asleep emphasized his age. The wrinkles in his face were deeper, and his fine white hair seemed so limp yet soft. Like the beautiful cherry of the old highboy, the character of his face had rippled with age.

During his lifetime, his grandfather was the one person he could count on, but he knew it wouldn't last forever. He thought about how strange his grandfather had been acting for the last few weeks. Tab saw him looking through old plans and asking him if he had seen various old tools that had not been in the shop in ages.

Even the conversation on the way into the city was a little odd. Benjamin seemed confused about how old Tabner was when he made the highboy, when Tab was the same age. The whole thing gave him a shiver as he sat and watched his grandfather sleep.

The hour passed by quickly. Tab gently shook his grandfather's shoulder. "Hey, Grandpa, sorry to wake you, but it's time for the reception."

He looked a little groggy as he tried to swing his feet around to the floor. "Boy, I sure needed that. I must have slept hard."

"You sure did. I thought you were going to shake the plaster off the walls when you snored."

"Really? I didn't hear a thing," he said as he grinned. "Well, let's get ready."

Tab was a fish out of water when it came to wearing a tie. He made several futile attempts before he finally gave in and asked the old master for direction. Benjamin grinned as he said, "See, you do have to get out more. It's just like carving; it takes time to master the fine art of tying a tie."

"I'm afraid I'm going to remain an apprentice when it comes to these things."

The auction showroom was packed with patrons sipping from wine glasses while trying to talk over the string quartet playing in the corner. Tab made a quick survey of the room to see if he was as out classed as he thought he would be. He was surprised there were people dressed in fine suits as well as jeans and sweaters.

He leaned toward his grandfather and said, "There's a couple of people here who look a little like bums."

"Don't be so quick to judge. One of them may be the richest person in the room."

They walked across the room to take their turn at a table full of different kinds of hors d'oeuvres.

Tab crinkled up his nose and said, "What do you think these things are?" He picked up a little triangular thing that looked like it was made with fifty layers of parchment paper.

"If I remember right, your grandmother used to call that *phyllo*, and there should be some kind of meat in it." He quickly picked one up and popped it in his mouth. "That was pretty good. You should give one a try."

Tab opted for the cheese and shrimp, but in the end took one of the phyllo things too. He wasn't adventuresome when it came to food, but anything that his grandpa thought was good like his grandma's food deserved a try.

They filled up their plates, feeling as though it may be the only food they would get to eat that night.

"Tab, I think I'm going to find somewhere to sit and enjoy this."

On the opposite side of the room from the quartet there were a couple of empty seats so they headed over and sat down carefully trying not to spill their plates. Tab was happy to sit off to the side and do a little people watching.

Sandy sat with Tab for a while, keeping him company. She made the observation about how his grandfather's face lit up when he talked about the highboy. Tab had mixed feelings about his grandfather's enjoyment when showing off the old dresser, and at the same time, he was irritated every time he introduced him. He hated all the attention and couldn't wait for the evening to end.

Sam was there too, so Tab was relieved to have a few people he felt comfortable talking to.

His grandfather had the ability to talk to anyone as if he had known them for years. Tab watched as he pointed out the details of the old dresser to a person sitting next to him. Sandy's comments were spot on. He really was having the time of his life.

Tab tried to make sure his grandfather got off his feet now and then, even if just for a few minutes. He even took another pass at the appetizers, loading up on the little triangular phyllo things for his grandfather. As they were nibbling on their selections, Tab said, "Hey, Grandpa, doesn't that man over by the quartet look familiar?"

"He does. Isn't he on TV?"

"I think he's on one of those money shows on cable."

A voice next to them said, "I think you're right. I don't think he's as smart as everyone thinks he is because he's often wrong more times than he's right. Take my advice, and listen to someone else if you want to keep your millions." He muttered something under his breath as he got up and walked away.

They both looked at each other and started to chuckle. Tab realized people were rather talkative.

They'd had a few pleasant conversations by the time the reception was winding down. Finally, Phil introduced another gentleman to them.

"Benjamin, I would like to introduce you to Mr. Robert Campbell. This is Benjamin Kirkman and his grandson, Tab."

His grandfather struggled to make it back to his feet.

"Oh, please sit down. You must be exhausted." Mr. Campbell pulled a chair around and sat down facing him.

"Thank you, you're right. I am a bit tired."

"Mr. Kirkman, I can't tell you what a pleasure it is to meet you. I have been an admirer of your family's work since I was a little boy. My mother had a Kirkman dining room set that she received as a wedding gift. She loved it, and I can say it was difficult to let my sister have it after my mother passed. I've been collecting fine furniture for years, and I'm happy to say I have a few Kirkman pieces of my own, but nothing as fabulous as this incredible highboy."

Tab was taking in every word and observing Mr. Campbell. It seemed obvious he was an important man from the way Phil introduced him.

He wore a fine suit and had perfectly polished shoes. He even had a handkerchief with his initials embroidered on it.

"Mr. Campbell, I'm so glad you're interested in old Tabner's work. I'm sure there are other pieces out there that are just as beautiful as this piece. Tabner and his father, Floyd, always used fantastic wood, but there's only one *first piece*, and there it is."

His grandfather insisted they walk over to the highboy. Mr. Campbell graciously helped him to his feet, and they walked slowly to the highboy.

His grandfather pointed out the finer points of the piece that made it a Kirkman and the things that made it uniquely Tabner's.

Tab had never encountered anyone like this before. It made him feel good to see someone of his status show so much respect for his grandfather. They went on talking about the old dresser as if it were a national treasure. By the time they were done, the room was almost empty.

Tab joined the two of them. Taking his arm, his grandfather said, "Mr. Campbell, my grandson, Tab, is an aspiring furniture maker like his namesake."

"Tab, your grandfather has invited me to visit your shop. I'm looking forward to seeing your work."

Tab found it a little hard to believe Mr. Campbell could possibly be interested in anything he would make. He couldn't imagine seeing one of the chairs he was working on having a place in whatever penthouse or mansion Mr. Campbell likely lived in.

"Thank you. I'm sure we're both looking forward to your visit."

His grandfather leaned on his arm. "This has been a great evening, but I think it's time for me to get off these tired old feet."

Tab knew that meant he really needed to go.

Mr. Campbell nodded with understanding and headed toward the door with them. They all said their goodbyes to Phil and entered the elevator. Tab and Mr. Campbell helped his grandfather.

"Can I give you a ride to your hotel?" Mr. Campbell asked.

Not wanting to impose, his grandfather shook his head, saying, "That's okay, it's just around the corner."

He replied, "It's no problem. My car should be waiting for me when we step outside."

Tab could hardly imagine what kind of car would be waiting and wondered if the driver has a cap like the ones in the movies.

Sure enough, as they exited the building, the driver stepped out of a long, shiny black limo in his black suit and cap.

Mr. Campbell said, "Really, it's no problem."

Tab put his hands on his hips and said, "Grandpa, are you really going to deny me my first limo ride?"

Mr. Campbell smiled and gave him a wink. "I think your grandson has a point. Accept the ride, for his sake."

They graciously accepted and drove around the block in style.

The next morning, Tab heard his grandfather tossing and turning in the next room as dawn filtered through the sheer blinds of his window. When he heard the shower, he decided to get moving himself. They were both dressed and ready to go hours before Clement's would even be open again for the morning viewing.

When they arrived in the lobby, they found it was nearly empty. Six o'clock in the morning on a Sunday was early, even in New York City.

They walked up to the front desk to ask where they could go for some breakfast.

"Good morning, gentlemen. How may I help you?"

"Good morning, young lady. We would like to have some breakfast," Benjamin said.

"Our restaurant opens in just a few minutes, or Starbucks is just around the corner."

"Grandpa, we have lots of time. Let's have a nice breakfast," Tab suggested.

"I would like that. Thank you, where—"

"Just to your right," remarked Tab as he motioned to the door.

Being the first in the restaurant, the server invited them to sit anywhere they would like. The aroma of Sunday morning's buffet had already filled the air, whetting Tab's appetite.

"Let's sit close to the buffet, Grandpa. I think you need to save every ounce of strength you have."

"I like your thinking, Tab."

Tab and his grandfather talked about last night's reception in between bites of their bacon and eggs.

"I can't believe how many people came to look at the highboy. You were like a rock star, Grandpa. Everyone wanted to talk to you, and I'm pretty sure I saw you sign a few autographs."

His grandfather let out a big belly laugh as he said, "I most certainly did not give any autographs … I was writing down our shop phone number for people who wanted me to look at their Kirkman pieces."

"Okay, I'll take your word on that," Tab said with a big grin.

"So, Tab, what did you think of Mr. Campbell?"

"He was very nice. I could sure tell he liked talking with you."

"I liked him too. He is a genuine person, and even though there was no doubt he was very wealthy, he made every effort to make you feel at ease. He also knows his antiques. It sounds like he is quite a collector."

"Do you think he's going to buy old Tabner's dresser?"

"I think he will!"

"So why is he going to come out and visit the shop? Do you have a project you think he might be interested in?"

"No, not exactly."

"What does that mean?"

"He's interested in seeing *your* next project."

"Why on earth would he be interested in anything I would ever make?"

"Well, first, he's interested in you."

"Me?"

"I told him that you were every bit as good of a craftsman as old Tabner."

"You told him that? Are you crazy?! I could never make anything like that highboy."

Tab's insecurities started to squash him down in his seat. He couldn't believe his grandfather would do that to him. He was perfectly happy doing whatever he needed him to do on their projects. He had never made anything completely by himself. Now he had a rich collector coming to look at his work.

"When is he coming? We don't have to put out the chairs I've been working on, do we? They would be pretty boring for him to look at."

"Come on, Tab. Don't get yourself so tied in a knot over his visit. Anyway, he's not coming for several months. I'm sure we can find something for you to work on by then."

Tab was relieved. "Maybe I can make one of those Duncan Phyfe nightstands."

"I've been thinking about a project for you to take on yourself. We'll get it sorted out in plenty of time."

The morning viewing at Clement's was packed with patrons. Benjamin talked to several more Tabner enthusiasts and loved pointing out the characteristics that made it a Kirkman piece.

Even Tab got in a few words about the work, and he was rewarded with his grandfather's smile.

As eleven thirty approached, they closed the room to viewing and Phil removed the ledger from the case and handed it back to Benjamin.

"Thank you so much for all you have done to help us out. I think you'll be surprised at what Tabner's highboy brings today."

"Well, if it meets the estimate, I'll be thrilled," said his grandfather with anticipation in his voice.

Phil smiled. "Well, I can't tell you how much, but we have some left bids and ... Well, that's all I can say. The auction starts at one o'clock, and surely it will be about five before the highboy is offered. We arranged a late checkout at the hotel in case you want to stay there and rest awhile."

"Thanks, Phil, this whole weekend has been quite an event. I think I want to experience the whole thing, though. Don't you think, Tab?"

"Absolutely! I'm looking forward to seeing what some of the other items sell for."

Tab wanted to sit in the back of the room so he could watch everyone bid. It was his first time at an auction and he wanted to see how it worked. They sat with catalogs in hand.

Tab made sure he had a pen so he could record what everything sold for. "So, Grandpa, how much do you think it will sell for?"

"It should go for at least $100,000. That's a lot of money, and I don't think it will get much more than that."

Tab said, "I think it's going to go for a little more. Remember what Phil said. I think he already has some big bids."

Most of the smaller pieces that were in the auction had been moved to make room for all the patron seating. The room started to fill up as the auction was about to begin.

Tab looked around the room to see how many of the people he had met were in attendance. The strange guy who sat next to them yesterday while they were eating was off to one side and wearing an old sweater. Several other acquaintances were scattered around the room. Tab noticed Mr. Campbell wasn't there. He wondered if the left bid was his.

Phil and the staff were taking their places while the auctioneer welcomed everyone. At the stroke of one o'clock, they started with the first lot.

As the auction progressed, Tab kept track of the price of each lot. Most items were selling for their estimates, but a few sold for considerably more.

Tab watched the sweater guy bid on several items. He was leaning against the wall and would swing his bidder's paddle whenever he wanted to place a bid. He thought it was so strange the way he seemed to have no emotion about winning or losing. He never wrote anything down like the other bidders to keep track of what they bought. Tab thought he seemed so out of place. The more he watched him, the more he saw. His pants looked like he had worn them for several weeks in a row. They were covered with stains, and one of his shoes was worn clear through its side.

He was getting a little concerned. Was he going to bid on the highboy? Would he take care of it? He wished Mr. Campbell would arrive soon.

Most of the auction had passed when Mr. Campbell walked in and sat down beside them.

"Hello, Mr. Campbell. I wasn't sure you were going to make it," his grandfather whispered.

"I wouldn't miss this for the world. I knew it would take about five hours to get to the end, and I wasn't going to bid on anything except the highboy. So, what number are we on?"

"Number 253 ... Forty-seven more to go," replied Tab, leaning forward so he could hear him.

The few remaining lots prior to the highboy were almost finished. The auctioneer caught their attention saying, "And our last item today is lot number 300. A magnificent Tabner Kirkman cherry highboy. I have several bids here at the desk, $140,000 looking for $150,000."

Tab looked at his grandfather with a big smile on his face.

Several bidders raised their paddles.

The auctioneer said, "I have 150, 160, now $170,000."

Tab was shocked to see the price climb so quickly. Two bidders were not bidding, Mr. Campbell and the old sweater guy.

The price kept climbing 180, 190, now $200,000. Still no bids from either of them.

"I have 200, do I have 210?"

Then old sweater guy swung his paddle.

"I have 210, do I have 220?"

Tab glanced over just in time to see Mr. Campbell nod his head.

"Now I have 220, do I have $230,000?"

Again, the old sweater guy swung his paddle.

Tab wasn't sure he liked the idea of this guy owning such a fine piece of his family's work. He swung his bidder's paddle again with disinterest. The thought of the man putting that old sweater in such a grand old dresser totally disgusted Tab.

After a long second, Mr. Campbell nodded.

"Now I have 240, do I have $250,000?"

The old sweater guy didn't move.

The auctioneer looked around the room. "Are we all done? I'm selling at $240,000. Are we all done?" He waited for a few more moments and then banged his gavel and said loudly, "*Sold* for $240,000!"

The auction house erupted in applause. The highboy had sold for more than double the estimate.

Mr. Campbell, looking satisfied with his purchase, looked over at them and said, "I get to take old Tabner home. That's fantastic!"

Tab scribbled a few numbers in his catalog and turned to his grandfather saying, "With the buyer's premium, that's $297,500. Unbelievable!"

His grandfather shook his head. "I never would have believed it." With a big smile, he stood and shook the new owner's hand. "I'm so glad it's going home with you, Mr. Campbell."

The auctioneer said, "That's the end of our sale. Thank you to all our buyers and our underbidders."

The old sweater guy headed straight for the desk to pay for the things he bought. Totally expressionless, he simply walked out the door. Tab was so relieved he didn't win the old highboy.

Mr. Campbell shook the hands of several other patrons before turning back to Benjamin. "Thank you for your help. I'm looking forward to getting it home."

Tab reached his hand out to Mr. Campbell to congratulate him.

Mr. Campbell shook his hand and said to Tab, "I'm looking forward to seeing what old Tabner inspires you to do."

Tab was still trying to understand how someone who just spent more than a quarter of a million dollars for this fabulous old dresser would have any real interest in his work. As much as it seemed improbable, he felt his intentions were nothing but genuine.

His grandfather looked at him and said, "Well, young man, it's time for the two of us to head home."

Tab was ready himself. While the auction experience made a huge impression on him, he also felt extremely tired from all the excitement. Like his grandfather, Tab had spent almost every day of his life at the shop. It was easy for him to take it for granted. For the first time, after having people like Phil and Mr. Campbell say things like tradition, legacy, next in a long line of craftsmen, he felt a real sense of pride in being part of the tradition.

As they drove out of the city, Tab and his grandfather sat quietly and thought about the events of the last couple of days.

"Let's take tomorrow off, Tab. There's something I want to do."

"You hardly ever take a day off, Grandpa. What's up? It must be something special."

"Oh, it is, Tab."

Tab waited for his grandfather to explain, but he said no more. So, Tab agreed to take tomorrow off but still wondered about his grandfather's cryptic request.

Chapter 3

The Challenge

T HE WEEKEND'S EVENTS WERE FRESH in Benjamin's mind as he buttoned his blue work shirt. The old highboy had sparked an idea, and he was eager to put his plan in motion. His daily ritual started with waking at his usual five o'clock. Most mornings his old knees were so stiff he could barely stand as he got out of bed. He hated to take medicine for anything, but for the past few years, he couldn't function without it. Most mornings he faced the steps with dread as he looked down from his second-floor bedroom.

Today was no different, and his knees snapped and popped with each step. He looked forward to his standard breakfast of two eggs, one slice of wheat toast, a cup of black coffee, and the morning's newspaper. By the time he finished his second cup of coffee, he was ready to head out to the shop after a fresh refill.

Benjamin's morning commute was just shy of ninety feet. Except for the three years he spent as a Marine, he had taken the thirty some steps almost every day of his adult life.

He unlocked the door with a well-worn skeleton key original to the workshop. As he entered, he reached for the light switch but momentarily stopped, and with a smile, he left them off.

To his right was the old drawing desk that Floyd made. It was angled about fifteen degrees to make it easier to see the top of the drawings. At the edge of the desk sat Tab's first project, a mug holder, proudly displayed against the rail that kept the drawings and drafting tools from sliding to the floor.

It was a block of wood about four inches square cut on the same angle as the table. There were four small dowel pegs that kept Benjamin's favorite mug centered on the block and GANPA written with black paint on the side.

Benjamin placed his coffee mug down in its honored place as he did every morning. He slowly lowered himself down onto the old wooden stool that had seen so many days of hard work. He reached to grab his mug and sipped his coffee as the sunlight crept in to fill the shop as it did all those years ago—the same sunlight that filled the shop when old Tabner made that wonderful highboy.

Not much had changed since old Tabner's days, except for the wood-burning stove that was replaced with a furnace and an air conditioner. The biggest change was the light switch he neglected to use this morning. The bright white walls of the shop were an important part of the natural lighting of the shop even today. There were just a few lights to fill in what the sun couldn't accomplish on a cloudy day.

By the time he finished his coffee, the light had filled the room. He turned back to the desk and grabbed his notepad to write down some ideas for Tab.

Benjamin had worked with his young apprentice every day for more than five years, and as much as he had praised and encouraged Tab, he never saw the spark of enthusiasm and pride for the work that he had done. However, yesterday was different. Benjamin thought he saw something spark in his spirit.

Their conversation at breakfast and Tab's excitement at the auction was something new. Benjamin knew he had taught him everything he needed to thrive in the business—everything but the one thing you can't teach: *passion*. He wanted to take advantage of that spark and give him a challenge. He wanted to give him something big—something he wasn't expecting.

He made a list of tools and then set off around the three buildings, collecting most of them as he went.

After about an hour, he had a pile of old dusty tools. Some tools hadn't seen the light of day for more than fifty years. Each old tool needed a little work, but he was sure they were still in working order. He headed toward the woodshed to see if he could find the pieces of the old six-foot power wheel and its old lathe.

The woodshed was two buildings in one. It was sixty feet by forty feet with a room on the south end that was about twenty feet wide. This was used for the saw shop. The north end of the shed was open to allow the air to move through the stacks of wood accelerating the drying process.

Much to his surprise, everything was there.

Benjamin looked up and said, "Thanks, Dad."

Benjamin had fond memories of the saw shop and woodshed. He was in grade school when his father and grandfather built it. He remembered every minute he spent with the two of them, from digging the trenches for the foundation to putting his handprints in the concrete floor. Even though he wasn't allowed to go up on the roof, he watched as every shingle was nailed in place from his second-floor bedroom window.

On this occasion, he was glad his father couldn't throw anything away. He was able to find almost everything he was looking for. He decided to wait for Tab to come in the following day to have him climb up to the loft. Some tools were still missing, and he wondered if that was where they were hiding.

When it was time to break for lunch, Benjamin walked back to the house to make himself his favorite lunch: goose liver on rye with spinach and sliced dill pickles and, of course, more coffee.

After lunch, he grabbed the paper and started on the daily crossword puzzle. After writing in a few words, he leaned back in his chair and closed his eyes as he searched his mind for the right word. After a few moments, he shook off the need to take a nap and took the last sip of coffee.

Much to his surprise, it was stone cold. He looked down at his watch and saw that he had been asleep for almost an hour.

"Well, not much work's going to get done around here if I'm sleeping on the job."

Benjamin's knees protested loudly as they snapped and popped again with every step as he walked his mug and dishes over to the sink.

After he had given everything a good rinse and put the dishes in the dishwasher, he reached for one of his medications in the cabinet. He shook his head with disapproval as he took another pain pill.

His arthritis was making it more difficult to be in the shop every day. After a long weekend in the city, his knees felt much worse, even his hands felt stiff and sore, but he still had unfinished work. He finished cleaning the kitchen and wiped off the table before heading back to the shop.

Back in the shop, he sat at his desk rubbing his aching hands as he searched the rack for a tube for a particular set of plans. They were very old and hadn't been used in years. After he pulled out several tubes, he finally spotted what he was looking for—a tattered old tube covered with a thick layer of dust.

Benjamin carefully removed the old plans, now yellowed with age. They crackled as he unrolled them, being careful not to tear them. He loved this old drawing and thought it had been too long since it was used. After studying the plans, he was sure his young apprentice was ready to tackle a project of his own. This project will help Tab understand how far his skills had come.

On a clipboard hanging on a nail next to his list was an inventory of wood in the drying shed. He looked through the list and found several cherry selections he would look at with Tab in the morning. He was very familiar with each stack, as he had restacked them several times as the wood was drying.

He looked over his tool list and made a few additions. Now, where would that hide glue and old glue pot be hiding? They had not used hide glue since the '60s, so he did not have much hope he would find it.

After looking on nearly every shelf, he decided he would have Tab look on the bottom shelf on Tuesday. His achy knees just wouldn't let him bend that far.

He grimaced as he stood up. His medication was failing him today. All this physical activity along with the weekend's events had gotten the better of him. He knew he had to be in the shop early in the morning, and the way he felt at the moment made it doubtful he could be at his best for Tab.

Despite his ailments, Benjamin fought his feeling of defeat and thought he would give his body what it needed most—rest.

Back inside the house, he slipped off his boots before heading up the stairs to his bedroom. He neatly folded his blue work shirt and trousers and laid them on the chair by the bathroom door. He splashed some water on his face to get the dust off from the woodshed and headed to bed.

He rubbed on some of his trusted horse liniment before he climbed under the covers.

Before he nodded off to sleep, he said, "I love you," and kissed the picture of his wife, Ellen, as he did every night. After a few moments, he was fast asleep.

The next morning, Tab got in his car to go to his grandfather's house.

Tab's day off had been a restless one. He had been committed to doing as little as possible, like watching a Yankees game on television, eating a big bowl of cereal, and taking frequent naps. His cereal turned soggy halfway through the meal, and he couldn't find anything worth watching on television. For some reason, the sandman was nowhere to be found.

He was a master at doing nothing when he was a kid, but it wasn't as easy as it used to be. His grandfather's work ethic had rubbed off on him, and he wasn't too happy about it.

He decided to spend his day off doing chores around the apartment. He cleaned the kitchen floor and did all the laundry. His favorite pastime was fussing over his car.

Tab traded his mom and dad's old car in on his twenty-first birthday and bought a brand-new silver Ford Mustang. He had stacks of magazines about Mustangs—anything he could get his hands on. This was one part of his life that felt right to him. Working on his car or taking it for a drive made everything seem all right for a while.

Like his grandfather, Tab's life was predictable and filled with unbroken routine.

Shortly after graduation, he moved into his own apartment.

Every evening he checked his mailbox for one of Isabella's letters. Her move to China was a big change in their relationship. She decided she would rather communicate through snail mail than email, but he turned on his computer regularly to see if by chance she had sent him anything. It didn't make any sense to him to use such an old method of communication, but she had insisted. He felt like he didn't have any choice in the matter.

He knew there must be something wrong with their relationship, but he wasn't able to get Isabella to talk about it.

Over time, her letters started to get shorter, and there were no more pictures. Months would go by without hearing from her.

It had been more than six months since her last letter. Tab sent one out every week, routinely like the rest of his life. Isabella's three-year contract was over three months ago. Tab convinced himself she had found someone else she'd rather be with and was never coming back. Another week had started so he wrote another letter hoping she might respond just in case.

He wrote about what he and his grandfather did over the weekend and how they missed hearing from her. As usual, he wrote how much he hoped to hear from her.

Tab placed the letter in the mailbox for the next day's mail pickup, hoping that he would see one from her too.

After finishing his microwaved dinner, he got a call from his grandfather asking him to be at the shop at 5:45 a.m.

"Why do you need me there at such an ungodly hour, Grandpa?"

"Tab, please. It's important."

"Are you sure? Are you okay? You're starting to worry me."

"I'm fine, I promise. It's just important that you're here at 5:45 tomorrow. Please don't be late, okay?"

At 5:45 a.m. on the dot, Tab parked his car in the usual place in front of the garage and walked toward the shop, kicking the stones as he went.

When he got close, he heard his grandfather's voice. "Good morning. Good to see you up before sunrise."

Tab walked over to the big shade tree at the side of the house where his grandfather was sitting on the picnic table thumbing through a little book.

"What on earth are you doing sitting out here in the cold reading a book?"

"This is going to be a very important book to you for some time to come."

"What is it that could be so important?"

"The old *Farmer's Almanac.*"

45

"Why would I need a *Farmer's Almanac*?"

"You know, this is a great little book. It tells you when it's safe to plant your corn, what the weather is going to be like next week, and, most importantly, it will tell you when the sun will rise and when it will set."

"Why on earth would I need to know that?"

"Old Tabner, like every farmer of his day, used his own *Farmer's Almanac* to tell him when the sun would rise, indicating when he needed to start his day in order to make the best use of every minute of daylight. He knew that he needed to get up with enough time to tend the farm animals, start a fire in the workshop stove, and have some breakfast just to be ready to get to work thirty minutes after sunrise. You see, every minute of sunlight was important in the nineteen hundreds because there wasn't any reasonable way to light the shop. You couldn't have open flames everywhere, especially in a shop full of wood shavings and sawdust. Look over at the shop. See how the sunlight is working its way down the side of the building? As soon as the light comes down to the side windows, it will be time to get started."

Tab looked at his grandfather with confusion. "What's going on? Can't we afford the electric bill, or are you thinking about going Amish?"

His grandfather chuckled and with a big grin he said, "No! Well, kind of." He reached over and put his hand on Tab's shoulder and gave it a little shake. "No, were not going Amish, but I do have a challenge for you."

"What kind of challenge?"

"Well, Tab, let's go inside and talk about it."

Tab walked into the shop and saw a pile of old tools lying on his bench. "Grandpa, what have you been up to?"

"I spent a little time digging up a few things to show you."

"I've seen most of this stuff before. What's so special about it?"

His grandfather waved him over to his desk where Tab saw several old drawings yellowed with age. "That looks like old Tabner's highboy!"

"That's right. These are the very sketches that Tabner drew for his highboy."

His grandfather stepped back to allow Tab a closer look. The plans were a thing of beauty in their own right. Every line and radius were still clear and only slightly faded around the edges.

"Wow, you can see every detail. It's all here! Look at the shape of the Queen Anne leg and the detail of the foot. The fan detail has two different versions, and it shows the shadow detail we saw on the auction piece. This is really cool!" Tab smiled and looked at his grandfather. "I had no idea you still had these."

"I thought you'd like seeing them. I could tell you were really taken with the beauty of old Tabner's highboy."

"It was so beautiful, and hearing the comments from everyone at the auction was incredible. The selling price of $297,000 was amazing. It got everyone's attention."

His grandfather smiled. "It felt really good, didn't it?"

"Grandpa, it made me think a little bit about being a Kirkman and of course being named after Tabner."

"I'm glad you feel that way because I want to give you a chance to get to know old Tabner a little bit better. Why don't you sit down and look over these old drawings, and I'll go make us some coffee."

After a few minutes, his grandfather returned. Tab held the door open as his grandfather handed him his coffee.

"Thanks. Wow, that's hot! You're always scalding me to death with your coffee." Tab took a tentative sip and walked over to the bench with all the old tools. "What are you going to do with these, start a museum?"

"All that stuff is about you getting to know old Tabner. I think it's time for you to take on a big project of your own. I want you to make a highboy like old Tabner's."

Tab sputtered as he sipped on his coffee. "You're kidding, right?" He put his mug down and fanned his mouth and then poked himself in the chest with his finger. "You want me to make a highboy like that unbelievable thing? Old Tabner was a real master. I can't do that."

"Tab, I want you to really get to know old Tabner. I think the best way for you to do that is for you to use his tools. I want to challenge you to make your highboy without any electricity. In the end, I have no doubt that you can make it every bit as beautiful as old Tabner made his."

Tab, shaking his head in disbelief, laughed. "You're kidding … That's crazy not using electricity."

"If you want to make a highboy that looks like old Tabner's, then making it with the same tools in the same shop is the best way to do it."

There was a long pause as Tab processed the challenge.

His grandfather waited for an answer, "Well, what do you think?"

"I think it's nuts!" Tab leaned back against the bench, looking down at the floor.

Over the past few months all he had heard about is how amazing old Tabner's highboy was. His grandfather held his work in such high regard. How could he possibly measure up? But there was a part of him, a sacred part of him, that stored his hopes, making him want to measure up.

His grandfather leaned against the bench next to him and put his hand on Tab's shoulder.

"Tab, you know I would never ask something of you that you weren't ready for. You *can* do this!"

Tab looked at him in dismay. "Okay … It's crazy … but it's okay."

"Great! Now here is another challenge," his grandfather said, handing him the *Farmer's Almanac*. "Just like old Tabner, you need to be in the shop in time to best use the daylight."

"No way! I need all the sleep I can get."

"Remember, that's part of the challenge … no electricity."

"Oh, man. You're killin' me!"

"Nonsense! It'll be good for you. Besides, I still need your help for all the other work. Let's have you work for old Tabner two days and with me the rest of the week. It's going to take a while to whip those old tools back into shape, and there are a few things we still need to find."

They both leaned over Tab's bench to look at the tools while sipping their coffee. Even though Tab was somewhat familiar with them, his grandfather refreshed his memory by recalling their uses and where they could be set up for Tab to use.

"That's most of them, but we're still missing a few." His grandfather held up a notepad. "Here is the list of all the tools. I think the rest may be up in the loft. Let's head out there and see what we can find."

When they entered the woodshed, Tab looked up at the loft to see a hodgepodge of equipment.

"Okay, Tab. I'll hold the ladder."

Tab positioned it and then hopped up and said, "What are we looking for?"

"We need to find a joiner plane. It's about five feet long and about six inches wide and made of beech."

Tab crawled around for a while, moving about and looking under odds and ends. "Hey, Grandpa, I found parts from my old swing set."

"Well, you never know when you might need one," his grandfather chuckled.

Tab shook his head as he looked under a canopy for the old two-seat glider that used to be out in the yard. "I think I found it." Tab pulled it out from under the canopy. "I would be hard pressed to call this thing a plane."

"Show it to me."

Tab stood it up against the railing, being careful not to hit his head on the rafters. "Is this it?"

Turn it around. "Yep, that's it. Are there two pegs with it that would fit in the holes at the end?" He pointed to the top of the plane.

Tab set it down and took another look under the canopy. "Nope, don't see any."

"That's okay. It'll take less time to make new ones than to keep looking for them."

"What else do we need?"

"The jack shaft for the lathe."

"What's that?" Tab asked.

"It's about three feet long and has two pulleys, one on each end."

"I saw it … It's over here." Tab pulled it up to the rail and said, "This is it, right?"

His grandfather nodded. "It's bolted to the ceiling and that big wheel over there mounted on the floor."

Tab held it up over his head to figure out how it all worked. "Okay, what about the belts? It looks like there must have been some kind of flat belt."

"I'm sure they're long gone. There were two one-inch-wide leather belts hand-stitched together. We'll have to have them made."

"Are you sure this is all necessary."

"Remember, no electricity."

"Did you ever use this thing?"

"No, I don't even think my grandfather used it. They had a foot-powered treadle lathe that my dad traded for the one we have in the saw shop now."

"Actually, Grandpa, I think it's pretty cool. I'm looking forward to figuring it out. Okay, what's next?"

"Now let's find the grinder."

"So, what does a grinder without a power cord look like?"

"Well, it has four legs like a sawhorse, a seat, and a foot pedal underneath."

Tab looked around and then spotted it in a corner. "Okay, I think I see it at the other end of the loft." He muttered, "Don't break your neck," to himself as he crawled over all kinds of old stuff, making him less sure-footed.

"What's taking so long?"

"Ouch! Oh, man, that hurt." Tab hissed as he banged his knee crawling over an old cabinet. "Hey! Give me a minute. I'm trying to climb over all this junk."

"Junk?! Remember, that's your inheritance you're talking about."

"Oh, that's what it is. Thanks for the clarification."

His grandfather chuckled. "Let me know when you're done getting familiar with everything up there."

"Okay, I think this is it, but there's no grinding wheel."

"When we stuck it up in the loft, your grandmother wanted to put the grinder's big sandstone wheel in her flower bed as an ornament."

Tab pulled it up to the loft railing. "I think that was more an act of love than landscaping." He wiped his brow as the perspiration trickled down his cheek. It must have been a hundred degrees up in the loft.

His grandfather looked up at Tab with a smile. "Yeah, you're right. That thing is really heavy."

"Are we done yet?"

"Just one more thing … a shooting board."

"What? You didn't tell me there were bullets involved."

"Knucklehead! No ... no bullets."

"I actually know what that is," Tab said proudly. "I picked up a woodworking magazine yesterday, and they actually showed how to use one."

His grandfather nodded with approval. "Very good, Tab. Very good."

"I think I stepped on it on my way over here. Yep, there it is." He bent down to pick it up off the floor. "Yuck! This thing is covered with cobwebs and mouse droppings. Come on, Grandpa. Is all this really necessary? This project is going to be hard enough using all these antiques, let alone no electricity."

"Of course it's necessary," barked his grandfather.

Tab felt a moment of irritation. If he didn't know better, he would've thought his grandfather planned that too. But truthfully, he did want to make a highboy like old Tabner's. And if his tools were what he needed to use, so be it.

Tab hung his head and said, "The things I do. Okay, let's get this stuff down."

Tab handed the plane down to his grandfather and grabbed a piece of rope to lower the jack shaft and grinder safely to the floor. He climbed down the ladder and said, "I'll come back and get the other stuff once we figure out where we're going to put it."

They walked back to the shop and put the plane with the other old tools.

"Let's go have an early lunch before we look at some wood," Benjamin said, feeling the need to sit and rest his legs.

Tab picked up their coffee mugs and headed toward the house.

"Would you like me to make you a goose liver and pickle sandwich?"

"No, thanks. I brought my own lunch," he said, relieved he didn't have to eat mushy liver and stinky pickles.

His grandfather grinned. They both knew Tab could not stand his grandfather's favorite sandwich and would always bring his own or offer to buy him lunch at his favorite diner.

Tab ran out to his car to retrieve his lunch—a bag of corn chips, beef jerky, and a soda. There was no chance he was going to eat that goose stuff.

Over lunch they talked about how they would set up the shop. They had another large project that would be done in a week or so. Tab would have to wait to rearrange the workbenches.

His grandfather suggested he spend some time getting his tools in working order before he started any new work.

Tab was starting to get the bug. This was going to be a big challenge in many ways; his mind was going a million miles a minute. He liked the idea of working with the old tools but had no idea how long it was going to take just to get the tools ready.

After lunch, his grandfather showed Tab the selection of wood for him to consider for his project. The boards were in a neat stack in the loft.

Tab climbed the ladder again to the top of the seven-foot high stack. His muscles strained as he pulled out a couple of heavy boards. He carefully slid them down to the ground. They were rough sawn, and it was hard to see what they looked like in the low light of the shed. His grandfather had him do the same with two other stacks.

"It's such a nice day. Let's pull them out into the sun and take a look," his grandfather suggested.

They laid them out on the grass and evaluated their color and figure.

Tab thought one of the samples was an instant front runner because its figure was very strong, but there was another board that was incredibly similar to old Tabner's highboy. "It's difficult to decide. I like them both," said Tab, scratching his head.

"Let me make some suggestions. You could make this piece in plain walnut, and it would be very beautiful, or you could make this out of highly figured maple like a violin back, and it would be overwhelming. You have to try to strike a balance between the piece's design and fancy wood. Sometimes highly figured wood looks better on a simpler design."

Tab agreed with both ideas. "I'll have to think more about it. Maybe later I'll plane the saw marks away to get a better look."

"That's an excellent idea."

Tab struggled to stand the twelve-foot boards on end to lean them back up against the stacks.

"You'll have to sharpen up one of those old planes before you can get a better look at the wood."

"Yeah, let's head back to the workshop. I've got to get the tools sorted out before I can get anything done," said Tab, eager to get started.

"What kind of priority would you put these in?" Benjamin asked his grandson, trying to get Tab to think about planning.

"I would take all the hand saws over to the hardware store and have them sent out to be sharpened. It may take a week or two to get them back. In the meantime, I can work on the planes and get them in shape. It may take some time to get them sharp enough to use."

Tab picked up a notepad and sat down in his chair. He sat for a while looking at a blank page, thinking about the challenge. Tab could tell his grandfather was really looking forward to seeing the project take shape. He didn't want to let him down and hoped his efforts would meet his grandfather's expectations.

"I think I'll start with sharpening the plane blades first," Tab began. "Some of them look a little rusty."

"Well, Tab, I never thought I would say this, but if you're going to start sharpening, you're going to have to start with a shovel."

Tab's mind went blank. "What?"

"A shovel. You've got to dig the grinding wheel out of the flower bed before that grinder's going to do you much good."

Tab laughed. "Right, the grinding wheel. I never thought I'd be using a shovel for this project."

Tab dropped his notepad on the workbench and headed for the garage for a shovel. As he walked around the front of the house, the old grinding wheel came into view. Tab had seen it a thousand times over the years and even remembered sitting on it in the hot summer sun eating an ice cream cone. What he didn't remember was how big it was.

The electric grinder in the saw shop had a six-inch wheel, but this thing was two feet in diameter. It was buried down to the hole in its middle.

Tab removed the dirt that held the wheel in place chunk by chunk. Then he tossed the shovel to the side and put his hands through the square hole to lift it out. He gave it a yank expecting to lift it right out, but it didn't budge.

He stood up and looked at it in disbelief saying, "Holy crap!" He bent over again and gave it another big tug. It seemed to do the trick. He lifted it out of the hole but set it back down before it crushed his fingers. "Man, how am I going to get this thing over to the shop?"

Eventually, he maneuvered it until it was upright so it was ready to roll to the shop. Its weight and gravity had other ideas. As Tab started to roll it toward the woodshed, it began to come to life. Without Tab's consent, it rolled down the slope toward the woodshed without him.

His grandfather came out to see what was taking so long just as Tab began to chase after the runaway wheel. There wasn't much he could do to stop it. The wheel was picking up speed on its way down the hill.

Tab stopped to avoid running into the shed, but the grinding wheel crashed with a spectacular sound.

His grandfather called down to him from the shop. "I see you got the wheel down to the saw shop. I think that's where you should want to use it too." He grinned and went back inside, not expecting the event.

Tab flopped himself down on the ground out of breath. He looked over at the wheel buried six inches into the side of the shed.

"Okay, dummy," he said to himself as he picked himself up and pulled the wheel out of the side of the shed, rolling it through the door and leaning it up against the wall. He went back into the woodshed and carried the rest of the grinder into the saw shop, finding a corner to put it in.

Tab could see how the two went together and in short order had the axle in the wheel, lifting it up into place. He sat on the seat, put his feet on the foot peddle, and gave it a push. To his amazement, the wheel started to turn.

After a few pushes of the wheel, it was up to a speed that was easy to maintain. He could see himself grinding his tools to perfection.

With the grinder ready to go, he went back up to the shop and gathered up the plane blades that needed to be sharpened.

He wondered what he'd gotten himself into.

Chapter 4

State Police

THE WEEK HAD PASSED QUICKLY as Benjamin watched Tab prepare his tools, and even though it was Saturday, he poured himself a cup of coffee and headed out to the shop. He did his best to try and slow down and get some rest on the weekends, but habit made it hard to stay out of the shop. Benjamin set his coffee cup in its usual place on the block that said GANPA that Tab made for him as a child.

He pulled the tube off the rack that held the drawings for their next project. The shop was going to get crowded with two projects going on.

Benjamin had estimated it would take many months for Tab to complete his challenge working by hand. Other work in the shop would take a bit longer now that he would be spending two days a week working on his project, but it would be worth the inconvenience to see Tab take on this challenge.

For years, Benjamin had pushed Tab to hone his skills; he could hardly wait to see the results. His young apprentice wasn't just talented; he was gifted. After a few years working full time, Benjamin knew Tab was going to be special.

He knew Tab struggled with his personal relationships, which kept him in the shop, but this project would be just the thing to give Tab the confidence to take over the business.

Benjamin knew that his time in the workshop was coming to an end; his old aching bones made it harder and harder to keep working. Lately, it was almost impossible for him to hold his hand tools without feeling the sharp pain of his arthritis.

The Kirkman reputation had been based on high-quality work for more than a century and a half. He couldn't imagine not working at his usual high standard, but with the help of the medication and ointments, he was going to do his best to be there for Tab.

Today was one of those tough days when the pain and weakness made everything difficult. Even the weight of a tube with the paper drawings for their next project was hard to hold onto. Benjamin uttered an, "Ouch!" as it slipped out of his hands and knocked his mug off its perch, spilling a full mug of coffee. The tube bounced across the wooden floor.

Benjamin Kirkman's smile was nowhere to be found today, as he pasted a rare frown in its place. The last thing he wanted to do today was to get down on his hands and knees to clean up the coffee splashed all over the floor, but the mess was his to take care of. He grabbed an old rag and gritted his teeth as he bent down on one knee to wipe it up.

As he wiped the floor, he looked under the desk and saw something written on the wall he hadn't seen before. His curiosity got the best of him despite his pain and discomfort. He managed to sit on the floor to get a better look.

To his surprise, the bottom of his desk was covered with all kinds of drawings. Benjamin could tell it was Tab's handiwork. He reminisced in his mind about Tab's swing set and Tab in his little apron.

Benjamin leaned back against the wall, his smile returning as a flood of memories rushed in.

His first son, Charles, would bring Tab to work with him on Saturday mornings. Charles wasn't much older than Tab is now. Benjamin had loved watching him work; it was so natural and effortless for him, and to have little Tab as a toddler running in the door wrapping himself around his leg and announcing, "I'm ready for work, Grandpa. What do you have for me to do?" It was a very special time.

Benjamin would get such a kick out of it that he always had something for him to do.

Tab's favorite job was drilling holes. Benjamin would draw an *X* in the middle of a scrap of wood, telling Tab he needed him to drill a hole right on the *X*, and he needed it done before lunch. Tab would take several blocks and head under Benjamin's desk, which Tab called his workshop, and got right to work.

The drill he used was an old gimlet. A gimlet was an old-fashioned tool that looked like a corkscrew. It threaded itself into the wood like a wood screw and cut the hole open to an eighth of an inch.

When Tab finished each one, he would bring it over to his grandpa to check his work. "Very good, my young apprentice. It's straight and exactly in the middle," Benjamin said, regardless of its truth.

Benjamin enjoyed seeing him so eager to please his grandpa. His wife, Ellen, had made Tab his own apron for his fifth birthday. Tab was so proud to look like his father and grandfather that he wore it everywhere, except school and church, often under protest.

On Tab's sixth birthday, Benjamin gave him his own toolbox complete with a saw, square, hammer, and set of auger bits. He could see that Tab could hardly contain his eagerness to start a new project. He worked with his father on a design to hold Benjamin's coffee mug.

Tab insisted on doing all the work himself so his grandfather would be, as Tab would say, "the mostest proud" of his young apprentice.

After a long Sunday afternoon working in secret—Benjamin wasn't allowed to enter the shop—and two tries at spelling GANPA, the surprise was ready for the big reveal. Benjamin remembered that Tab could hardly stay in his seat during Sunday dinner, too full of anticipation to present his gift.

After everyone finished their peach cobbler, Charles announced, "The apprentice has something to present to his teacher." With that, Tab jumped off his chair and ran into the living room where he had hidden his masterpiece.

In a flash, he ran back in and plopped an old shoebox down in front of Benjamin. Some string was tied around it like a ribbon. "It's for you, Grandpa. I made it just for you. It's for your coffee cup." He jumped and fidgeted. He could hardly stand how much time it took for Benjamin to open it.

Benjamin finally got the triple knot untied and slid the top off the box. He pulled the creation out of the box and looked at it with pure delight.

Benjamin held it up and examined it like he would one of his own creations. Tab watched as he held the little block of wood full of plane marks and wooden dowels sticking up all at different angles. The whole thing was stained a dark walnut and varnished with shellac. The most important part was the white painted oval with the inscription in slightly crooked but boldly painted letters: GANPA.

He looked down at his little apprentice and said, "In all my life, I've never received a gift more special than this. Did you make this all by yourself?" Trying to keep a straight face, he looked over at Charles.

"You bet he did! I tried to help a couple of times, but Tab wouldn't have it. He insisted it was going to be his and his alone," confessed Charles.

Tab nodded his head and in his little high voice exclaimed, "I'm really getting good, aren't I?"

Benjamin laughed along with the rest of the family and rustled up Tab's hair. "You'll be taking over for me soon, won't you?"

Tab nodded his head again. "Uh-huh."

"You know, Tab, I think I know exactly where I'm supposed to use this—at the edge of my desk." Benjamin got up from the table and said, "I can't wait to see how it works. Let's go, Tab."

With Tab running and skipping to keep up, the two of them were off to the workshop with the rest of the family following closely behind. Tab bounced alongside him across the driveway and into the shop.

Benjamin sat his gift on his drawing bench and then placed his mug on it. "It's perfect! I couldn't have done any better myself."

Tab hugged him with a big squeeze and said, "I love you, Grandpa."

Benjamin returned the gesture with his own big squeeze. "I love you too, Tab. You really made me feel special."

Tab went to bed that night saying he was the best craftsman ever, except for his grandfather, of course.

Those were the happiest times for Benjamin. Charles and Elizabeth were so happy together. Having his son working with him and his little apprentice on Saturdays made life perfect. But Benjamin's life took a few curveballs over the next few years that tested his faith.

He had never given much thought about his wife's annual doctor visits. Shortly after Tab's sixth birthday, Ellen and Benjamin's lives were turned upside down with her diagnosis of breast cancer. Ellen had fought a heroic battle, but within six short months, she was taken from him. Benjamin had barely spent more than a day away from his bride during their thirty-three years of marriage. Benjamin was overwhelmed with grief.

His friends from church did their best to console him, but it was his little apprentice that day by day would begin to chip away at his despair.

He and Tab had a special relationship. Tab could hardly stand to wait until Saturday when he got to go to work with his grandpa. Charles arrived with Tab early, insisting they arrive at the shop at the same time as his grandfather.

Benjamin would often refer to Tab as his little life saver.

As time marched on, life became more bearable. Sometimes he felt guilty when he found himself able to concentrate on his work. Little by little, a new normal crept into his life.

One part of his life, however, never changed. Benjamin never failed to say, "I love you," to his photo of Ellen before he went off to sleep.

It was Tab's seventh birthday when they received a very special visitor, Benjamin's second son, Ronny. Ronny was a load master on a C-30 Hercules cargo plane.

Tab referred to Uncle Ronny as "a real life army hero!" Ronny was modest about his accomplishments, but little Tab was right; his uncle had spent two tours in Afghanistan. Benjamin could tell Ronny enjoyed spending time with Tab and loved how he would stick to him like glue, wanting to hear every adventurous story.

Benjamin loved both of his sons and hoped he could get Ronny back in the shop someday. This particular trip home he talked about making the army a career, dashing Benjamin's hopes of having his family close. He knew Ronny felt he never fit in at the shop, saying often he just didn't have the gift that his father and brother had. He always joked that the birds didn't even like the birdhouses he made as a kid.

Being in the service of his country in all kinds of new places was the right place for him.

Ronny's visits were few and far between, but Benjamin appreciated every moment he was willing to spend with the family. Benjamin always wondered if he was too hard on him. Did he expect too much of him? Did he push him away?

Despite Ronny's long absences, the Kirkmans' business was doing well. Benjamin and Charles were busier than ever. The small shop had a steady stream of commissions. Many of them were repeat customers, some even second generation.

Charles's carving skills were remarkable, and Benjamin loved working with his son. It was gratifying to see that the Kirkman shop was securely in the hands of the next generation.

One of their commissions was for a shaker-style hutch. Mrs. Weber wanted to match the hutch to her photos exactly. She explained that her grandmother had gotten the hutch, table, and chairs for a wedding present.

When her grandmother passed away, her things were divided between her two granddaughters. They both hated to split up the set, but they both wanted it. So, they decided to flip a coin, allowing the winner to choose which piece they wanted. Her sister took the hutch and gave her the table and chairs.

Mrs. Weber explained how it just didn't feel right not having them together, so she wanted the Kirkmans to make a replica.

Benjamin remembered the day she came to see the finished piece. She walked through the shop door and was delighted with what she saw, but the longer she looked, the more overwhelmed she became. Tears filled her eyes. She smiled at Benjamin as she pointed to a scratch on one of the doors. She said, "The mark is here! How did you know?"

Benjamin said, "We could see it in the photo."

"My grandmother always called it a witness mark. She was a little sad to see that my sister and I had put this big scratch in the door when we were playing tag in the house on a rainy afternoon. The tall wrought iron lamp stand fell against it and left that big mark. After she sat us down and explained how important the hutch was to her, she said the two of us, my sister and I, were forever linked with it. The scratch was a witness to the two of us playing that day."

Benjamin loved presenting new pieces to his customers, especially those who were longtime patrons of the Kirkman shop, like Mrs. Weber. For him, having a connection over the generations between the Kirkmans and their customers' families was special.

Benjamin's daughter-in-law, Elizabeth, had her own twist on the business. She was getting very good at identifying older Kirkman furniture. She loved traveling around the countryside going to antique stores and estate sales looking for older pieces. Sometimes she would come home with something she could actually fit into her little car.

It was at one of those country auctions that she ran into a young Phil Scott. She was excited to share what she had learned with someone who was so interested in the Kirkman workshop.

After a few years, she had a nice collection, to the point that she had to make a decision to stop buying or find a way to start selling off a few things. She had way too much fun finding and buying to ever stop. When Phil began working at Clement's, she was thrilled to send a few of her treasures his way.

As the years marched on, Tab's play on Saturdays turned into real work. Benjamin helped Tab make his first chair when he was only ten years old, and he carved his first claw and ball on a table leg at the ripe old age of twelve.

As Tab approached his sixteenth birthday, Charles and Elizabeth planned a weeklong trip around Massachusetts and Maine. They were going to an auction in Boston that had several Kirkman pieces and then to Maine to see a table and chairs she'd seen on the internet. Of course, every antique store they could find along the way was part of the plan too.

Tab's enthusiasm for antique stores had left him long ago, and he had expressed his happiness to stay with Benjamin.

Tab wrinkled his nose at the idea of taking a tour of every antique store in New England.

Benjamin laughed. "We'll have our fun, won't we?"

Tab had packed everything he needed for the week and moved into his dad's old bedroom.

Tab and Benjamin saw them off early one Saturday morning. Elizabeth was anxious to get going. She wanted to arrive in Boston just as the auction house opened at ten o'clock in the morning. That gave them time to view what they were interested in and then have part of the day to explore the city.

Benjamin shoed them toward the van and gave them both a hug. "Don't worry. We'll take good care of each other."

They sat there for a while with Elizabeth's door open. Finally, she shouted, "Come on, Tab. You know I can't leave without a proper goodbye."

Tab rolled his eyes as he reluctantly walked over to give his mother a hug goodbye. She gave him a good squeeze and whispered something in his ear.

Tab gave her a peck on the cheek and closed her door.

As they drove away, she pointed at Tab with a stern look on her face.

Tab raised both of his hands and yelled, "I promise."

Benjamin smiled at Tab as he waved him into the house.

Benjamin had big plans of his own. He and Tab were going to spend the week together and then head into New York to see a Yankees game. Benjamin loved the Yankees and was pleased Tab was looking forward to the game too.

They had great seats along the first base line. Benjamin had a longtime customer who had season tickets. Once in a while, when he couldn't make a game, he would enjoy giving his old friend tickets.

Tab had his fill of popcorn and peanuts and was a little annoyed with the Cleveland player who hit three foul balls in a row right at them.

Benjamin loved it. "It makes you feel like you're part of the game, doesn't it?"

Tab wasn't amused. He proposed the upper deck for the next game.

Then a thunderous crack split the air ... a long fly ball. The stands erupted with loud cheers as the ball sailed over the left field fence. Tab and Benjamin cheered and jumped to their feet.

Benjamin said, "There's nothing sweeter than a homer to win!"

After the game ended, they gathered their things and headed out with the rest of the crowd. On their way to the exit, Tab asked to stop at the team store to check out the hat selection.

"Your mom and dad are going to be home before we are," joked Benjamin. He was happy to let Tab look around on such a special occasion.

After looking at every single hat in the store, Tab picked the one hat that looked like it had been left out in the weather for a year, run over by a few trucks, then chewed on by some animal.

Benjamin said, "Are you sure you want that ratty-looking thing?"

"It's perfect."

Benjamin grinned. "Sure, I think it looks great too."

Tab proudly put his new hat on his head and checked it out in the mirror on the way out of the store.

On the drive home, Tab fell fast asleep in the back seat. When

Benjamin pulled into Tab's driveway, he expected Charles and Elizabeth to already be home and unpacking the treasures they collected. Unexpectedly, the house was dark, and they were nowhere to be seen. So, he drove through the U-shaped drive and continued on to his house, which was only five minutes away. Tab could spend the night with him and go home after school.

As he turned into the driveway, there was an unfamiliar car parked in the drive. He heard Tab stir.

It was hard to see who it was in the dark, but as he drove closer, he could see that it was a police car. Benjamin could feel his heart jump up to his throat.

"What's going on, Grandpa?" Tab asked, wiping the sleep from his eyes.

Benjamin didn't answer. He put the car in park and stepped out of the car. Tab slowly followed as he stumbled out of the car.

A tall, slender state police officer approached them and said, "I'm looking for Tabner Kirkman."

Tab looked concerned, but Benjamin knew he hadn't done anything wrong.

Benjamin stepped forward and said, "I'm his grandfather, Benjamin Kirkman."

The officer looked very somber and said, "Sir, I have some bad news."

Benjamin stopped him in midsentence and said, "Which one?"

The officer said, "I'm sorry, sir. It was both of them."

Tab was looking back and forth between the two of them. "What did you say? Grandpa, what did he say?"

Benjamin stepped back as if the officer's words had punched him in the gut. Benjamin stood there with his mouth open, unable to say anything.

The lieutenant looked over at Tab and said, "Young man, it is my sad duty to tell you that your mother and father were killed in a car accident this afternoon."

Tab turned, doubling over, and an ear-piercing unintelligible cry left him as he slid to the ground.

Tab's cries jolted Benjamin back to reality. He knelt down to try to be of some comfort to his little apprentice, knowing at that moment there was nothing he could do to lessen the pain.

Benjamin looked up at the officer and noticed he was having a hard time keeping his composure.

The officer said, "Sir, I am truly sorry about your loss. Please take my card, and when you're able, call me, and I'll do my best to answer your questions." He reluctantly turned and got back into his car and drove away.

Benjamin slipped the card into his shirt pocket and hugged his sobbing grandson. His own grief overwhelmed him.

They sat there together in the driveway, in the dark, until Tab could make his way up the steps to the house. Benjamin took him up to his father's old room.

Tab dropped himself down on the edge of the bed and burst into tears again.

Benjamin sat down beside him, still searching for the right words. He knew his presence was more important than anything he could say.

Finally, Benjamin uttered, "Tab, I know this is horribly unfair, and there isn't anything I can say that will make you feel any better, but what I can say is, we will get through this together. We'll … Well, we'll figure it out together."

Tab leaned against him, paralyzed with grief.

"Why don't you lie down and try to get some sleep. There's nothing we can do until morning."

Tab nodded and kicked his tennis shoes off, scooching himself toward his pillow.

Benjamin pulled back the covers for his young apprentice. Once he was settled, Benjamin stroked his tear-stained cheek, his own eyes wet from grief.

Tab curled himself into a fetal position. Exhausted by the ordeal, Tab's grief was mercifully interrupted as he fell into a deep sleep.

Benjamin left Tab's side and headed down to the kitchen. On his way down the stairs, he heard the phone ring. The answering machine picked up, and Benjamin heard his son's voice. "You have reached Kirkman and Son. Please leave a message after the beep."

He dropped to his knees. "Oh my God!" He burst into tears at the sound of his son's voice. The full weight of his loss crashed down upon him.

Benjamin sat in the middle of the kitchen floor for nearly an hour trying to regain his composure. He knew he had to make some painful phone calls. The first call had to be to Elizabeth's parents, then Ronny, and then everybody else.

There was never a good time to get bad news, and it was getting late. He wiped his eyes with his handkerchief, sat the phone on the kitchen table along with his address book, and started to dial.

Halfway through the first number, he put the receiver back down. "Oh dear, what am I going to do with Tab?" Ronny was single, no home to speak of, and lived far away from anything Tab knew, and he potentially could be called away at a moment's notice. Elizabeth's parents also lived far from anything familiar to Tab. Benjamin knew in his heart that Tab belonged with his grandpa Kirkman and no one else. They would need each other to heal from their loss.

He felt overwhelmed by the idea of raising a sixteen-year-old, but he knew that it was the best thing for Tab to stay with him. Eventually, he pulled himself together.

Over the next few hours, he talked to a dozen family members and close friends.

He looked in on Tab before he dragged his tired body down the hall to his room to get ready for bed. He stripped down to his boxers and laid down on his bed.

Before he turned off his light, he looked over at the picture of his wife and said, "Take good care of them, Ellen. I love you."

He turned off the light and said a quiet prayer. "Jesus, give me the strength and guidance to comfort Tab, and help us through our grief. Amen."

Benjamin sat on the floor for almost an hour. He heard Tab pull up in his car and was surprised to see him so early, especially on a Saturday.

He struggled to his feet just as Tab entered the shop.

"Grandpa, are you okay?"

"Oh sure, I was just looking at your handiwork under my desk."

Tab bent down to see what he was talking about. "Oops, sorry about that."

Benjamin said, "I want to show you something." He led him over to the other side of the shop and pointed under the bench. "That's my handiwork."

Tab bent down and saw the little stick figures drawn under the bench top. Unlike Tab's drawings, his were mostly war themed.

Tab said, "What's with all the tanks and planes dropping bombs?"

"Remember, when I was growing up, it was during World War II."

Tab laid on the floor and took it all in. "It looks like you spent many Saturdays in the shop with your grandfather too."

Chapter 5

Willy Ross

TAB WAS SURE HE HAD the old grinder figured out. How hard could it be, anyway? It was simple—a round abrasive stone that ground away the steel blade as you pressed it against the wheel. However, theory and practice seemed at odds.

The first obstacle was the wheel. The years had not been kind to the old sandstone. It had eroded in the flower garden. Tab could see the surface was different where it had been underground for forty years.

That meant he would have to redress the surface of the stone before he could start grinding. Dressing the large grinding wheel was a dirty, noisy, and tiring process. Tab had to use a super hard steel bar to flatten the surface of the wheel by holding it tightly against the wheel. He had done this many times before, but never with a wheel so big and while he was pumping it with his foot.

He poured water into the trough that sat just under the wheel to help keep the steel from getting hot and the wheel from getting clogged with metal as it ground away the blade.

He was finally ready to start grinding. Tab held the first plane blade up to the wheel. It was hard at first to hold it steady, but after a little practice, he was surprised how well it worked. It wasn't as fast as his trusty electric grinder, but he didn't miss all the sparks and how hot it made the blades.

By midday, his hands were wrinkly and stained from the dirty water used to lubricate and cool the tools. At least he had all the tools he needed to get his project started.

Tab returned his sharpened plane blades back to the workshop where his grandfather was working.

Noticing Tab's hands, his grandfather laughed. "I haven't seen you so pruney since you spent too much time in your kiddie pool over there in the driveway," he said as he pointed out the shop window.

"I think my hands have had it for today. I think it'll take until tomorrow for them to dry out anyway."

His grandfather nodded in agreement. "I think you've had a great first day."

"Thanks. I'm glad to get that out of the way. I'm ready to get something to eat. Can I take you to the diner today, Grandpa?"

"That sounds great, Tab, but first let me finish the last of these spindles for the Windsor back chairs. I only have three to go."

"No problem. I'll just sit here and watch."

His grandfather turned back to his work. He was sitting on a little elongated bench, known as a shaving horse, that had a block at the end with its tail end sticking down through the top. He would place the end of the spindle under the block, pushing it against the tail end with his foot. Tab knew this made the block rotate down onto the spindle, holding it firmly in place. Then he took his drawknife with both hands and started to shave the end of the thin square stick of ash into a round, tapered slat that would fit into the chair seat.

Tab loved to watch him work. His grandfather made quick work of the first one and released it with his foot and put another in its place.

"How many of those things do you think you've made?"

"Oh, gosh ... You know ... I have no idea. Many hundreds, anyway." He continued shaving the slat. The drawknife made a funny whistling sound as it cut through the wood. As he leaned forward to complete each stroke, the bench creaked.

The hint of a memory nudged Tab's mind.

"How old is that bench, anyway? It's pretty cool. I'm sure I remember my dad using it."

"Of course he did! He replaced the foot pedal when it was worn out." Grabbing the last slat, the shavings made a tight curl and then leaped onto the floor as they sprang off the edge of his drawknife. With a few more strokes, he was finished. "That's about all these old hands are going to take today."

"Let's find a place to have dinner."

He could see his grandfather's hands were getting worse by the way he flexed and rubbed them after the last slat. Tab jumped to his feet to grab the broom before his grandfather got the chance.

"While I clean up, Grandpa, why don't you go ahead and wash up, and I'll meet you at the car."

He grinned. "You got a deal."

Tab offered his hand as his grandfather swung his foot over the side of the old bench. He gladly grabbed Tab's hand to steady himself and rocked himself to his feet.

"Thanks, Tab. I'll see you at the car."

Tab watched as he walked toward the house. Although his grandfather tried to make light of his discomfort, he knew it was getting harder for him to work with each passing day.

After cleaning up, Tab locked the door with the old skeleton key and waited in his car.

His grandfather soon appeared in a clean blue work shirt.

"Okay, let's head for the diner," said Tab.

"No, I think I want to go somewhere else for a change."

"Really?"

"Those pruney fingers of yours made me think of fish for some reason." Tab chuckled. "Do you have a place in mind?"

"Seafood for sure, but no franchises. Let's find some kind of mom-and-pop place."

"You need to tell me where you're thinking. There's nothing like that around here."

"Let's just do a little exploring. I'm sure we'll find something. Just head south. We've got all evening."

Driving his car was Tab's favorite pastime. A drive down to the coast with his grandfather was an added bonus. Most of the time Tab wouldn't stop anywhere, but with his grandfather, it was different. Tab felt more confident around him. They weaved their way along the west side of the Connecticut River until they reached the sound.

Suddenly, his grandfather spotted an old root-beer stand that had a sign that read:

Monday's Special
Baked Flounder w/ Hushpuppies
and a Large Drink
Only $9.99

"This will do! Pull in right here," he said, motioning to the run-down little diner.

Tab turned the car into the parking lot.

"Are you sure you want to eat here? This place looks like it's seen better days."

"Look at all the cars. That's a good sign. I think we should give it a try."

Tab waited for a departing car and pulled into a parking spot right in front of the door. The old diner, clad in faded stainless steel was a relic of the '50s.

"Tab, you're going to love this old place."

When they entered, Tab said, "Wow! This is really cool! Look at all the polished stainless steel and red vinyl."

His grandfather pointed at the only available seats.

After being seated at the vintage booth, a young waitress promptly came to take their order. "Hi, what can I get for you gentlemen?"

They ordered two specials, a Coke for Tab, and an unsweetened ice tea for his grandfather. Then the girl bounced off to place the order.

"This place really brings back the memories."

"Have you been here before?"

"No, not this place, but these old diners used to be everywhere. The doughnuts were over there, and the apple pies were over there, and you used to play your favorite records from this old thing." Benjamin pointed to the little jukebox at the back edge of the table.

Tab flipped through the list of songs and laughed. "Chubby Checker?"

"He was pretty popular back in the '60s."

The waitress brought their drinks. "Your dinners will be up in a minute."

After she left, his grandfather remarked, "She's kind of cute."

Tab cut him off and said, "Let's not get this started. Besides, this is too far from home." Tab glanced at the waitress's swinging ponytail and girly figure. "Anyway, I don't think she's out of high school."

"Okay, okay, I just wanted to see you find a nice girl to go out with."

"I'm just waiting for the right girl to come along." Tab tried not to think of Isabella, but she surfaced in his mind.

"I know, I know, I just don't want to see you alone. Your grandmother and I were already married and had two kids by your age."

After a few minutes, the waitress bounced back with their food.

Tab was grateful for the interruption.

They sat quietly as they ate their dinner. Tab wasn't sure how long the quiet contentment would last.

If not his love life, the conversation would always get around to his social life.

"Have you heard from Willy Ross lately?"

Willy was Tab's best friend since first grade. He was the one person who helped Tab feel normal after his mom and dad died. After Tab moved in with his grandfather, Willy would show up at his house and insist they go out and do something.

Whether it was with their skateboards or ringing doorbells at two in the morning, Willy was a pro at getting into mischief, and Tab played along.

His grandfather would often nudge Tab out the door, encouraging their mischief rather than risking Tab be cloistered in the house and further withdrawn from the world.

The summer before their junior year, Tab's grandfather made arrangements with Willy's parents to send them to summer camp for two weeks.

Northern Maine was a world away for two kids from the suburbs. Tab had no idea there were so many stars in the night sky. They were lucky to see more than a few back in West Hartford. They also spent time canoeing and fishing. Tab and Willy had never done anything like that before.

Camp was a turning point for Tab. It was the first time away from his family, and he had the time of his life.

After they returned from Maine, Willy began to have different ideas about the kind of mischief he was interested in. In their neighborhood, Celeste Sabatini was the most beautiful thing Willy had ever seen. Willy couldn't believe this Italian bombshell could be interested in him, but she was, and she couldn't get enough of him.

But there was a problem—a big problem. Celeste had an identical twin sister who did everything with her. Her name was Isabella.

While Willy didn't mind being seen with two beautiful girls, which he announced on more than one occasion, his goal was to spend time alone with Celeste, and that meant that Isabella had to go.

This was just another one of Willy's schemes to get Tab and Isabella together, and it didn't go unnoticed. Tab was anything but thrilled about it.

This didn't stop Willy and Celeste from inviting Tab wherever they went. He was officially invited to occupy Isabella.

One night when summer vacation was almost over, Willy made arrangements for Tab to sleep over.

Willy's house was a short skateboard ride for Tab. When he arrived, Willy rushed him inside.

"What's going on?"

"Nothing." Willy glanced out the window, trying to appear innocent.

Tab shrugged and went out the back of the house to shoot baskets. After a few minutes, he wondered where Willy had gone. He looked around and saw two shadowed figures approaching.

It was the twins.

Tab watched Willy meet them outside in secrecy and then joined them. He felt irritated by Willy's deception, but knew he'd hang out with them anyway.

Willy and Celeste led the way down the road, Tab and Isabella falling in step behind them.

Tab knew something was up. He said to Isabella, "Do you have any idea where the two of them are taking us?"

She gave him that sarcastic as-if-you-don't-know look and didn't say a word. Her long, thick black hair flowed like silk in the night breeze.

Tab looked back at Isabella's closed expression and wondered what the three of them were up to. He was starting to feel a little uneasy.

After another block and a left turn, he knew they were heading for Willy's aunt's house.

Willy's aunt spent the summer at her cottage in the Berkshires. Willy would go over to her house three times a week to water her plants.

Willy pulled the key out of his pocket. As they entered the dark house, he said, "Don't turn on any lights. I don't want the neighbors to know we're here." He led them up to the second floor and the balcony overlooking the backyard.

Celeste was eager to get the night started. She opened her bag and pulled out eight cans of beer. Willy and Celeste both opened one and took their first sip, urging Tab and Isabella to have a beer too.

They both reluctantly picked one up and popped the top.

Tab took a sip and swished it around. Warm foam instantly filled his mouth. He did his best to swallow and not let on how awful he thought it was.

Isabella just sat there in steely silence.

Willy said, "I have an idea! Let's play truth or dare."

Celeste said, "That's a great idea!" as if she were reading from a script.

Isabella said, "Oh, let's," in a sarcastic tone as she looked at Celeste with eyes that could kill.

Tab didn't know what to say, so he just shrugged his shoulders.

They started out asking each other easy questions, and then it was Tab's turn.

"Truth or dare?" Celeste asked.

Tab thought for a moment and said, "Dare."

Celeste got an evil grin on her face, and then said, "I dare you to go in the bedroom with Isabella and make out with her for five minutes."

Isabella just looked at her sister with a stone-cold glare.

Isabella stood up, grabbed Tab by the hand, and led him into the bedroom across the hall.

She gave him a shove, and he landed on the bed. She stood over him and pulled her pink gloss lipstick from her pocket, laid on an extra thick layer, and slid it back into her pocket.

Then Isabella reached out and grabbed his shirt collar with both hands. She bent down and planted a greasy kiss on both sides of his face. Then she went to kiss him on the lips.

Tab pushed her away and said, "What are you doing?"

"I'm just giving you what the three of you want."

"What are you talking about?"

"The three of you conspired to get the two of us together, so I'm giving you what you want!"

"Don't you mean the three of you?"

Isabella stopped and said, "You're not part of this?"

"No! I don't want any part of this," Tab said as he wiped her lipstick off his face with his sleeve.

She sat down on the bed with him and said, "I thought we were going to stay at our friend Jen's house."

"That sounds familiar, We're staying at Willy's."

She smiled and said, "Let's get out of here."

They walked back out to the balcony and saw the two lovers with half of their clothing on the ground, so engrossed with their lust that they were oblivious to their audience.

In their embarrassment and disgust, they turned and headed for the door. As they reached it, Tab stopped, and said, "Hey, where are we going?

Isabella said, "I can't go home, not without Celeste, and anyway, Mom's probably drunk with her creepy boyfriend. I don't want to be anywhere near him."

"I'm not sure what I should do either." Tab looked into the living room and said, "We could just sit and talk. I promise I won't try anything if you promise to keep that pink grease in your pocket."

Isabella laughed, and they found a couple of chairs across from each other.

"So, what's your story? You're so different from your sister."

Isabella threw her hair back and looked away from Tab. "I sure hope so."

"I'm sorry. I didn't mean to offend you."

"It's okay. Actually, I'm glad you see the difference between us."

After a brief period of silence, Tab said, "So, your mom is dating some creep?"

"Yeah, I can't stand him. I don't think I've been undressed by someone's eyes so many times. He's such a jerk!" She leaned forward and lowered her voice. "Once I was in the shower, and I heard the bathroom door open. I thought it was Celeste because we share the same bathroom and are always in each other's space. When I shut off the shower and pulled back the curtain to get a towel, he was leaning against the sink looking at me. No apologies—he was right where he wanted to be. I grabbed the towel and ran out. I told Celeste, and she said he had made a pass at her when Mom wasn't home."

Tab couldn't imagine such an invasion of privacy. "Did you tell your mom?"

Isabella looked out at the night with bitterness. "I promptly got a slap in the face for trying to ruin something good for her. I think my mom is addicted to men or something like that. She has men over all the time. I can't stand hearing the sounds that come out of her room."

Tab didn't know what to say. He couldn't imagine what her life was like, but he was starting to get an idea where her edgy side came from.

"Anyway, I think even though Celeste doesn't admit it, she likes the attention from men too."

"Was she always like this?" Tab wondered.

Isabella shook her head. "Something happened to Celeste when Mom started having her affairs. She started to dress like mom and loved it when men would whistle and pay attention to her. I've asked Celeste about it many times, but she won't talk about it. I don't think she can be happy without a man's attention."

"Well, I know for a fact that Willy is a good guy," Tab told her.

Isabella ignored his comment. "The more I see Mom and Celeste and the kind of men they have around, the more I want to be as far away from them as I can. And as far as men are concerned, they're all pigs—big, fat pigs. No man is going to touch me—not now, not ever."

Tab said, "Ever? That's a really long time."

"You're damn right!"

Tab said, "I'm sorry you had to go through that. It sounds like this guy really is a creep. What about your dad? Isn't he any help?"

"Not really. When we were in sixth grade, my mom found out that my dad was cheating on her, and she threw him out. She thought she would get revenge and had a few affairs of her own. Somehow that made her hate my dad even more. She just sort of lost her mind and made it impossible for him to be around us."

They sat there again not saying anything, and then she said, "So, I hear your mom and dad died."

"No, they didn't die," Tab said in a calm voice.

Isabella said with surprise, "Oh my God, I'm sorry. I thought Willy said they were dead."

"Oh, they're dead all right, but they didn't just die. They were killed. They were murdered." Tab's voice lowered to a growl by the end of his comment. It was difficult to keep the anger from his heart.

"Murdered? What do you mean they were murdered?" Isabella's eyes got as big as saucers.

"Some idiot drank half a keg of beer and fell asleep at the wheel. He slammed head-on into my parents' car going 80 miles an hour, and killed all three of them."

Isabella put her hands over her face, "Oh my God, that's horrible … I had no idea … Oh, I'm so sorry."

"The police officer said they had a combined speed of 140 miles an hour. He said they were killed instantly, and I hope to God they were. But the thought that I can't get out of my mind is, did they see him coming? Did they know they were going to die? And that jerk who was going to kill them was fast asleep, oblivious to the violent act he was about to commit."

Tab remembered the day after the accident and how he insisted that he and his grandfather go down to the police station for more information. They met with the lieutenant and listened to the awful details of the last moments of his parents' lives.

Afterward, Pastor Richards met with them at the funeral home. He spent the rest of the afternoon talking about the events of the next few days, which had marched forward with military precision. Go here, do this, make that decision.

Tab felt that it was all kind of sick how the funeral seemed to trivialize the whole thing; all those enduring kindhearted people expressing their sympathies and how sorry they were for his loss.

Tab said, "I think it's been harder on my grandfather. He misses them terribly. It took him almost a year to get my dad's voice off the answering machine. And my grandmother, she died when I was about six. I see him sometimes talking to the picture of her on his nightstand.

After seeing him carry such grief around every day, I'm not sure it's worth it."

"What do you mean, worth it?"

"Why get married, have kids, have a family, just to feel so awful when they're taken away from you. I think you're better off just being by yourself so you never have to go through that kind of pain."

They sat there quietly thinking about the evening, absorbed in their own thoughts. Tab sat with his eyes closed, leaning back in the overstuffed chair.

Isabella eventually broke the silence, "I have an idea!"

Tab was half asleep when he replied. "What kind of idea?"

"Now, hear me out. You're not looking for a girlfriend, and I don't want to have anything to do with creepy men, but it turns out that we're the perfect couple."

Tab sat up in his chair and gave Isabella a puzzled look. "Couple?! What are you talking about?" He tried to keep the sarcasm from his tone but failed.

She sat forward in her chair. "Yeah, it'll be perfect. We hang out together and have fun together, but there's no hugging, kissing, or holding hands and definitely no sex."

Tab cocked his head to the side, suspicious of her intentions. She had been anything but friendly to him for as long as he had known her.

"Come on, Tab! What do you have to lose? We're going to spend the next year tethered to Willy and my sister. I can't be home without her, and I can't stand being with her when the two of them are slobbering all over each other. And I think you're not happy being used like you are right now."

She had a point; he wasn't very happy with Willy, and he wasn't looking forward to telling his grandfather about what happened tonight. Isabella's idea was very interesting, and he was intrigued with the possibilities it presented. One thing it would do right off the bat would be to make his grandfather feel better about Tab having more friends. So, he agreed. "Sure, why not."

They talked about what they might do together to make their relationship convincing, but their words became fewer and fewer until they had both fallen fast asleep in their chairs at opposite sides of the room.

The next thing Tab saw was a flickering reddish light behind his eyelids, of which he couldn't make much sense. When it became too bright to bear, he opened his eyes and shielded them from the intense morning light that streamed through the windblown leaves outside the large picture window.

He looked around the room, not sure where he was for a moment. He saw a somewhat familiar form with long black hair on the chair across the room.

Now it was all coming back to him.

He had spent the night talking with Isabella while Willy and Celeste rolled around on the balcony with each other.

Isabella was still fast asleep, and he was anxious to leave Willy's aunt's house before someone found out they were there.

Tab saw a vase with long peacock feathers to the left of the fireplace. He quietly crept over and plucked one out of the vase. Then he knelt beside Isabella's chair and gently stroked her cheek with the feather.

To his surprise, she quickly reached up and grabbed it right out of his hand. "What are you doing?"

Tab jerked his hand back, "Yikes! How did you see it? You had your eyes closed."

She said, "Around my house, you have to have eyes in the back of your head, especially with Mom's creepy men in the house."

"Let's get out of here before Willy and your sister make their appearance."

Isabella nodded and said, "Okay." She searched the floor for her shoes and grabbed her things as they hurried out the door.

But they hadn't taken more than a few steps when Isabella stopped to run a brush through her long black hair.

Tab looked at her a little irritated, "What are you doing? Let's get out of here."

She quickly put him in his place with a loud, "Shush! Don't start telling me what to do. That's another rule."

Once on their way again, Tab walked quickly, as he wanted to put some distance between them and Willy's aunt's house.

Isabella yelled, "Slow down! Where are we going anyway?"

Tab turned back to see Isabella out of breath. He stopped for a moment to let her catch up, but in that moment, it came to him. He wasn't with Willy anymore. He was with a girl—alone with a girl for the first time in his life. He looked at Isabella who was standing in front of him with her hands on her hips.

"I'm sorry."

"I'm okay. I just want to know where we're going." Isabella continued to huff and puff, gasping for breath.

Tab thought for a minute and said, "Let's go to the diner my grandfather likes. They have great waffles."

"I don't have any money, do you?"

Tab said, "Sure, my grandpa always makes sure I have a twenty-dollar bill for emergencies. I think two hungry people on a Saturday at seven thirty in the morning is a real emergency, don't you?"

"Okay with me, Tab. Are you sure your grandfather won't get mad at you?"

"No way. He would never get mad at me for feeding a pretty girl breakfast."

"Don't go there, Tab, or you'll be on your own."

"Okay, okay, I get it. I was just giving you the business," he said as he gave her his big Kirkman grin.

She waged her finger at him as she started to say, "I'm not kidding," but she couldn't keep a straight face and gave into Tab's infectious grin.

Tab and Isabella spent the first of many days together comparing notes about their broken lives. Isabella was a frequent visitor at the Kirkman home, and Benjamin said he was delighted to see his grandson with such a nice and respectful young lady.

The twosome became regulars on Saturday mornings at the diner with a fresh twenty-dollar bill supplied by his grandfather. Now that Isabella was gone, Tab could barely stand to sit in their booth.

Chapter 6

The Key

BENJAMIN HAD BEEN AT HIS bench for more than an hour when he heard the rumble of Tab's car pulling up to the garage. He glanced over at the clock as his young apprentice entered the shop. The expression on Tab's face couldn't hide his lack of enthusiasm for this early arrival.

Benjamin said, "Good morning ... You're late."

"What do you mean, late?"

"Didn't you look at your *Farmer's Almanac*? You should have arrived at six fifteen a.m. sharp. The light in the shop has been good for more than an hour now."

Tab opened his mouth to say something and then just shook his head. "Six fifteen? I don't think so. That's just not human."

Benjamin got a kick out of watching Tab drag himself in so early. He thought this project might just cure him of being late for work, among other things. "If you're going to work on your highboy, maybe it's best to start with some coffee. You look so tired. You should go to bed early like I do."

Benjamin asked, "What are you going to do first?"

"Well, I'm going to lay out my wood and make some decisions about how I'm going to use each board."

"Okay, where are you going to do it?"

"Well, I think I'll lean the boards up against the woodshed to see what they look like in the sun. I guess that's as good a place as any."

Benjamin nodded. "Would you like some help?"

"I've helped you do it before, but I've never done it myself, so yes, any recommendations you have would be great."

Tab grabbed a piece of chalk and the old Stanley three-foot folding ruler, part of his new old-school tool kit.

"Don't forget your list of materials. It's the only way you'll know if you have all the parts you're going to need."

It took a lot of effort to get all the heavy boards off the stack and propped up against the shed. Tab worked up a pretty good sweat. Benjamin was out of breath and sat on an old maple stump and wiped his brow with his handkerchief. "Those old boards are a lot heavier than they used to be!"

"Stay right there. I can get the rest." Tab wrestled the last of the heavy twelve-foot boards up against the woodshed.

The low morning sun made the figure in the wood stand out boldly, making it easy to see all the defects as well.

Trying not to repeat himself, Benjamin asked, "What are you going to do first?"

"Mark all the defects."

"I agree. Then what?"

"I think I'll choose the best side of the board," said Tab thoughtfully.

"That sounds good. Take your time. This step is very important. I think I'm going in for some more coffee. Do you want some?"

Tab nodded and said, "All you can bring!"

Benjamin gingerly walked back to the house, feeling every bit of his overexertion. This time he didn't hesitate to find one of his pain pills. He knew he had overdone it, and this was the only way he was going to make it through the rest of the day.

He sat for a few minutes before pouring Tab a giant mug of coffee and the usual for himself. The downhill slope back to the woodshed was painful. The pressure on his knees was nearly unbearable. After he handed Tab his mug, he headed straight for the old maple stump.

"Are you okay?"

"Oh, sure! It's just that downhill slope. It kills my knees." He rubbed them, trying to get some relief.

Tab had several boards graded with chalk, circling all the knots and cracks and anything else that might take away from the beauty of his highboy.

Benjamin watched as Tab methodically examined each board. After Tab had marked all the boards, he stood back from the shed to get a better look at each board as it stood in front of him. Seeming a little bit intimidated by the next step, he looked over his shoulder, "How am I doing so far?"

"You're doing fine, Tab. Keep going," replied his grandfather, reassuringly.

Looking at his material list, Tab measured several boards for length and width with his old ruler. After a few tries, he marked several boards with his chalk writing *side* on one and *drawer* on another.

"So, you've made some decisions."

Tab turned and saw Benjamin looking over his choices. "Well, what do you think?"

Benjamin said, "I think it's very nice wood—yes, very, very nice."

Tab waited. "I was hoping for more feedback."

"This is your project, Tab."

Tab started to arrange the boards into categories: sides, drawers, and trim.

While Benjamin was happy to guide Tab when necessary, he really wanted Tab to take his project by the reins. Benjamin stood up to leave, but thought it was time to give Tab a piece of advice before heading inside. "Think about this. It's a showpiece ... Use the best wood ... Don't worry about using a small part of a board if that's all you want from it."

Tab looked closely at each of the cherry boards leaning up against the shed and replied, "How do you make that kind of decision? There are so many choices." He grabbed one of the boards and turned it around and leaned it back against the shed, and then did the same with several others.

As Tab turned to look at him again, Benjamin made his way around the corner of the shed to avoid his questions.

Eventually, Tab caught on and spent the rest of the morning making some preliminary cuts with his newly sharpened handsaws.

Benjamin watched through the shop window as Tab made steady

progress. He was glad to see that Tab appeared more confident about his decisions.

Tab had the long boards lying out on sawhorses in the yard outside the woodshed. Using his handsaws, he cut them into manageable pieces and marked them with chalk to remind himself where he was using each piece. By the end of the day, he had everything cut and ready for the next step.

"Okay, Tab, tools down! Your day is done. You have about fifteen minutes before you start to lose light. You should get your boards back into the woodshed for now, and tomorrow you can move them into the shop."

The next morning, Benjamin heard the wheels of Tab's Mustang screech as he came to an abrupt stop in the driveway. Out of breath, Tab entered the shop and said, "I hope you have plenty of coffee. This six fifteen in the morning stuff is for the birds."

Benjamin laughed. "No, Tab. It's six thirteen today. Didn't you look at your almanac?"

He dropped his chin to his chest and headed for the kitchen. "I definitely need more coffee."

Tab sat with his giant coffee mug in hand, taking sip after sip as he focused on his material list with his sleep-deprived eyes.

Finally, Benjamin asked, "Are you going to work on anything other than that coffee?"

Tab looked up. "Well, if I was making this in the twenty-first century, I'd know exactly what I would do."

"Well, the good news is that you do the steps in the exact same order—but by hand."

"I just don't see how I'm going to plane a ten-inch wide board flat and then make it all the same thickness without plugging something in."

Benjamin grinned at his young apprentice. "The old wooden plane you sharpened with the slightly rounded bottom is called a scrub plane. Its rounded blade lets you remove wood very quickly so that you can correct any twist or warp in the board. Then you can switch to your smoothing plane to clean it up."

"That sounds like a lot of work."

"I'm not going to lie to you. You're going to work up a good sweat."

"Great." Tab tossed his notepad on the bench. "I'll go and get a few boards. How many do you think I can do in one day?"

"Maybe two or three. Depends on how much you want to sweat."

Tab spent the whole morning pushing the old plane up and down each board. The sound the thick curls of wood made as they leaped out of the top of the plane was a cross between whistling and tearing. After a few hours of planing, Benjamin could see Tab was getting tired.

"It sounds like your plane needs to be sharpened. It's not singing the same tune as it was when you started."

Tab looked at the rounded edge of the blade. "Wow!" He sat down on his stool and wiped his brow with his sleeve; his shirt was sweat-stained. He looked at his hands; both had blisters starting at the base of each thumb.

"Ouch! Those hands look pretty beat up. Maybe you should take a break."

Tab nodded. "I think I'm done planing for the day. I'm not going to be much good for the rest of the week if I don't take care of my hands."

"I think you're right. Why don't you clean up your work space, and I'll make us some lunch."

"You got a deal. I'll see you in a few minutes."

Benjamin felt a little pity for Tab and knew his standard goose liver and pickle sandwich wouldn't cut it today. Luckily, last night he had cooked meatloaf using Ellen's famous family recipe. There was no doubt in his mind it would be a treat for Tab.

He had their plates of food on the table with a big glass of milk for Tab and Benjamin's ever-present coffee.

While they ate, Tab talked about how hard it must have been to build things before power tools. Benjamin knew Tab was starting to get a real feel for how extraordinary old Tabner's highboy really was.

"Did you ever have my dad make a highboy?"

"No, he never did, but he did make something special." Benjamin sat back in his chair and stared out the window for a moment. "Pretty special," he repeated.

Tab's question brought back a flood of memories as Benjamin began to smile. "We had this young couple with more money than sense. They took a tour of one of those old hunting lodges up in the Adirondacks, and they fell in love with the furniture in the dining room. They wanted us to make a copy of an enormous hutch. It was a style that was often made in southern Germany called a *hunt*."

"Why was it called a hunt?"

"On each of the door panels were carvings of animals that had been killed in a hunt and were being offered as a gift. It's hard to explain."

"I know exactly what you mean. I saw something like that in one of the auction catalogs Phil gave me."

"Good. They had a book they got with a picture of the room. The man also took a picture of his wife standing in front of it. That's all we had, so your father thought if he knew how tall she was, he could figure out all the measurements. He worked on the drawings every night for nearly a month and showed them to the couple. We gave them a crazy price because it was going to take a long time to do all those carvings. I never thought they would go for it, but they did with one condition." He looked at Tab. "They wanted it in four months. I was against it, but your mom and dad needed the money, so we accepted the challenge. Everyone in the family was in on it, even you."

"I don't remember it at all."

"You were only about a year old when you started to come to the shop with your dad." He smiled again. "Your father's carving produced countless big walnut chips. I remember your grandmother was constantly digging those out of your mouth. You know, I think I might just know where there might be a photo or two."

He disappeared for a few minutes to retrieve some old photos from his desk.

"Here's one of your father carving a pheasant motif on one of the panels. You can see just off to the side another finished panel with a rabbit carving. I remember that someone said that Michelangelo could look at a piece of marble and see the figure inside. All he had to do was remove the unwanted pieces. That's the way your father was with carving. It was really something to see."

Tab took the picture and stared at it for some time. Then he looked at the next photo.

"You can see the body of the cabinet is complete, and your mom is starting the French polish. It was the best finish to keep the crispness of the carving. Your mom was really good at it." His voice slowed as he finished. He watched as Tab examined every detail.

"I didn't know Mom worked in the shop!"

"Well … She did a few things. Her college art classes came in handy sometimes. She was great at finishing, especially French polishing." He handed him another photo. "Here's another one of your dad, and look, that's little Tab with his grandfather."

Tab's face scrunched as he peered closer. "What on earth am I wearing? I look like I'm one of the Simpsons with that yellow thing on. How could they do that to me?"

Benjamin leaned over to look at it again, and with a big grin, he said, "I think that's a trundle bundle. I remember your grandmother thought you were so cute that day that she couldn't stop giving you kisses. She would make a funny sound and kiss you on the neck, and you would laugh and laugh."

Tab slapped the picture down and said, "Next."

"This last one, I really like. It's of the three of you standing in front of the newly finished hunt. Your dad was really thrilled with the way it turned out and so were the clients."

Tab stared at the photo for a long time. Benjamin sensed Tab's mood change as he shrunk down in his chair. Benjamin stood to clear the lunch plates from the table.

"Do you miss Grandma as much as I miss Mom and Dad?"

Benjamin set the plates in the sink, putting both hands on the counter, his head drooping with feelings of loss. With their backs to each other, Benjamin replied in a soft voice, "I miss all of them, every day."

"Me too."

With a sigh, Benjamin tried to turn his attention to the cup and coffee mug from the table. Tab took the photos and stacked them neatly and placed them in the middle of the table. His feeling of loss grew with every moment.

"I think I need to go home and take care of these blisters. I don't think I can do any more work today anyway." He scooted out the door before Benjamin could think of something to say.

Benjamin stood alone quietly, trying to avoid the feelings that were welling up inside him. "Got work to do," he said to himself as he finished cleaning up the kitchen.

Taking the pictures from the table, he looked at each one again before placing them back in the envelope and returning them to the little desk in Ellen's room.

Benjamin never liked to go in this room. It was where Ellen spent her last days. In recent years, he made an effort to keep the door open. He even hung new pictures of Tab's friends on the walls to go along with Ellen's favorites.

Sitting in the desk chair, he allowed one picture in particular to catch his eye—Isabella.

She was such a bright spot for the two of them. She hadn't just helped Tab but had helped him too.

He remembered the day he had opened Ellen's door for the first time in years.

It had been a quiet day in the shop when Benjamin heard a knock at the shop door. He looked out the window and saw the familiar thick black mane of Tab's friend Isabella as she leaned her bike up against the workshop.

Benjamin opened the door and said, "Isabella, what a surprise!"

"Mr. Kirkman, can I come in?"

"Of course. You don't have to knock." Benjamin held the door for her. "To what do I owe the pleasure?"

She said, "I'm looking for Tab. Do you know where he is?"

"He and Willy are skateboarding in the park, but he'll be home for dinner."

"Oh, okay," she said in a disappointed voice. "Would it be okay if I hung out here with you?"

"It would be my pleasure. I would love the company. Please make yourself at home." He could tell she was upset, and he was happy she felt comfortable waiting for Tab at the shop. Tab had told him about her home life, and it made him sad to think this beautiful little girl had gone through so much.

"Isabella, why don't you sit right here, and I'll show you how I carve the claw over the ball on this chair leg." He had all the chisels and gouges laid out in front of him like a surgeon ready for an operation.

Isabella spent the afternoon watching every stroke of his chisel.

She looked fascinated. "You make it look so easy. The two of them look exactly the same."

Benjamin smiled and sliced through the wood with his gouge as the eagle-like feet took shape.

When the sunlight in the shop started to dim, Benjamin said, "Okay, Isabella, I think that's about all I'm going to do for today. It's time to clean up."

Isabella jumped up and grabbed the broom. "Let me do it. I want to help."

"Well, thank you. I appreciate that." In a few short minutes, they had the shop clean and ready for morning.

"Now, I think I'm going to go sit on the porch for a while. Would you like to join me? Tab should be home pretty soon."

Isabella nodded, and with a big smile, she said, "Great. Let's go."

As they walked the short distance from the shop, Benjamin asked her how her college applications were going.

"I have it narrowed down to two schools—one in Oregon and the other in Washington state. My grades and SAT scores are good enough to get in, but I'm hoping I get lucky enough to get financial aid from at least one of them."

"Isabella, if it's okay with you, I'm going say a little extra prayer for you tonight. I don't believe in leaving something as important as this to luck."

Isabella smiled and nodded her head. "I've never had anyone pray for me before." Benjamin held out his hand as she walked up the steps to the front porch. "Don't be so sure. I've told my Ellen about you."

"Who's Ellen?"

"She's Tab's grandmother. She died when Tab was little. I talk to her every night and tell her about her little Tab. I have her picture on my nightstand. It gives me strength to see her face when I go to bed every night."

"I'm so sorry. You must really miss her."

"Thank you. I sure do."

They sat on the porch swing to pass the time. They made some small talk as they waited for Tab to come home.

It was around five thirty when Benjamin said, "I think I'll get dinner started. Would you like to stay and join us?"

Isabella quickly said, "I would like that very much."

"Do you need to call your mother to let her know you're staying for dinner?"

"No, I know for a fact she doesn't want me home anytime soon."

Benjamin was a little surprised by her statement. It made him sad to think she didn't feel wanted. "Okay, then I better get started."

Isabella said, "I would love to help you. Can I?"

"Your help would be greatly appreciated."

Their time in the kitchen was delightful. Benjamin loved having the company; the house felt lonely without his family.

They heard the pounding of Tab's footsteps running up the back steps into the kitchen right on time. Isabella and Benjamin looked up from cooking together to see Tab's surprised face.

Benjamin said, "Hi, Tab. We've been waiting for you."

Tab asked, "What's been going on here?"

"Isabella is teaching me how to make one of her family's Italian delicacies. Wash your hands, and find a seat. Dinner's ready."

That evening they had a fun dinner together, joking and enjoying each other's company. It was a little bittersweet watching his two youngsters having so much fun together. Benjamin thought how it was before that horrible day and how unfair it was for Tab. Elizabeth and Charles would have enjoyed watching the two kids together.

Isabella had brought Tab back to life. When she was around, he wasn't just going through the motions. Whether Isabella knew her effect on them or not, Benjamin wanted to find some way to show his gratitude.

After the meal, Benjamin grinned and winked at Isabella, saying in a teasing manner, "Tab, since we cooked, you get to clean up."

His young apprentice grumbled a little bit but smiled as he started to gather up the plates.

Benjamin walked with Isabella through the living room. "There's something I want to show you."

He led her into the small side room. The walls were covered with family photos, and the bed was covered with stuffed animals. Isabella looked around at everything.

"I don't come in here anymore. There are just too many memories here. I arranged this room for Tab's grandmother when she was going through chemo. Tab's mom framed all these pictures and hung them so Ellen could see them from her bed."

Isabella said, "It makes me sad to be in here too. I'm so sorry."

"It makes me a little sad too, but I think it's time to leave the door open and raise the shades so the light can come back in like it did when Ellen was here."

Isabella studied the pictures, pausing at one of little Tab with an apron and a big toothy grin. She bent over to look closer and said, "Look at all those freckles!"

Benjamin laughed. "He had a lot of them."

Her amusement faded as her expression tinged with sadness. Benjamin wondered if she was thinking about her own family.

He opened a drawer in a little desk and searched around until he found a key tied to a long leather shoelace.

"Isabella," Benjamin said, "I have something for you." He took her hand and placed the key in her palm. "This is for you to use any time, any day, if you should ever have a need."

Isabella looked up at him with disbelief and started to speak.

Benjamin placed his index finger up to his mouth and made a quiet shushed sound. "This is between you and me. No one else needs to know, not even Tab for now."

Isabella hung the key around her neck and flipped her long black hair through and tucked the key inside her shirt. She gave Benjamin a big hug and whispered a quiet *thank you*.

In a whisper, Benjamin said, "I know my Ellen would approve." He was looking forward to telling Ellen about this before he said his evening prayers.

Isabella whispered another *thank you* and then said, "I think I'll go help Tab."

Benjamin watched her disappear into the kitchen. It felt so good to have Tab and his friend in the house. He could see how good the two of them were for each other.

Over the years he did his best to hide his worries from Tab. Aside from hoping that Tab could continue the family business, Benjamin was afraid that if something were to happen to him, Tab would never recover and would spend the rest of his life alone.

If there was anyone in the world he knew who could pull Tab out of his shell and help restore the joy he had before his parents died, it was Isabella.

Chapter 7

Growing Up

"RAIN THREE DAYS IN A row! I can't see what I'm doing. Are you sure I can't turn on the lights?"

"You know the rules of the challenge. If you want to turn on the lights, you'll have to stop working on your highboy."

"How can you see well enough to carve those claw feet?"

Benjamin grinned. "Do you know how many times I've carved these? I can do it with my eyes closed."

Tab plopped himself down on his stool. His whole body ached from days of planing all the boards for the highboy. The highly figured wood made the work much more difficult because he had to figure out what angle he had to hold the plane as he pushed it across the board. It took all his strength and concentration.

Tab pressed himself back to his feet and pulled another board from the pile. "I'm going to move to the bench closest to the window. Maybe the light will be better there."

"I was wondering when you were going to do that. The light gets too flat the farther you get away from the window."

"How long were you going to wait before you said something?"

"You're doing fine, Tab. You'll just have to figure out how to use the natural light to your best advantage. Sometimes you want flat light that won't make strong shadows. Today the light is shining right through the side windows. That gives you more direct light and strong shadows. That will help you see the bumps and hollows in your boards."

Tab took his long, straight edge and set it across the length of the board. He bent down on one knee so he could see the sunlight under the straight edge. "All right! That's much better." Where he could see no light, he made a squiggly mark with a piece of chalk. He clamped the board to the bench and started to plane off the high spots.

After about an hour, he had the first side flat. He flipped the board over to start on the other side but was interrupted by the phone ringing.

Tab stood and stretched his back, thankful for the interruption.

"Kirkman and Son, how can I help you?"

"Hello! I would like a matching set of birdhouses, painted red for my living room, and I need them by the end of the week."

Tab snickered at the familiar voice. "Would you like bluebird houses or a big old box for an old crow like you?"

His grandfather turned to look at him in disbelief. Tab started to laugh uncontrollably as he kidded his old friend Willy.

"Well, you old goat! How ya doin'? I haven't heard from you in almost a year!"

"Hey, Tab, it's good to hear your voice," laughed Willy on the other end of the line.

His grandfather shook his head and turned back to his work.

"What's going on, Sergeant Ross, or is it general now?"

"It's still sergeant. I wanted to let you know that we're going to be in town for a few days, and we want to see you while we're there."

"Of course," said Tab. "I had no idea you were dropping in."

"Yeah, Celeste, the kids and I are all coming home for a surprise sixtieth birthday party for my father. My mom wanted us to come, but I wasn't sure until the last minute if I could get leave. Oh! And she wants you and your grandfather to come too."

"When are you coming?"

"On Saturday. See you in two days! Got to go … bye." Tab could barely hear him over the sound of screaming kids.

"Wait! Willy! Ahhh! He hung up. Hey, Grandpa, Willy's coming home! He's going to surprise his mom and dad for his father's sixtieth birthday."

"Well, that'll be a treat."

Tab felt a rare spark of pure happiness at the chance to see his old childhood friend again. His head filled with all the things he wanted to do with Willy while he was in town.

Over the years, Willy and Celeste kept in touch, the proud parents sending photos of their children. Tab's grandfather even framed the pictures and hung them on the wall in Ellen's room with all the other family photos.

When Willy's oldest began walking, the videos were all over his Facebook page. Willy was clearly having the time of his life, and Tab could see that Willy was a natural at being a dad.

Their paths had taken them in different directions, but Tab hoped they would always be best friends.

The next two days were torturous. The June sun streamed through the windows, forcing Tab to work twelve-hour days. He would get home exhausted with just enough time to nuke a frozen dinner and watch something on cable before passing out.

On the night before Willy's expected return, Tab's mind was overactive, despite his exhaustion.

After channel surfing around the stations three times, Tab turned off the television in disgust. "Can't they put something worth watching on at least one of the 150 channels?"

He sat for a while thinking about looking through the auction catalogs again, but a box of old photos on the kitchen counter caught his eye.

He sat at his kitchen table looking at one photo after another. The pictures his grandfather showed him at lunch the other day of his mom and dad in the shop stuck in his head. He didn't remember any of it. His grandfather said he was only a year old, so it made sense.

The thing that bothered him the most was that he couldn't remember some things about his mom and dad. He looked through all the photos in the box, trying to find out what color his mom's eyes were.

"Blue. They were blue," he said to himself after finding a close-up.

He thought about what it would be like to go to his own father's birthday party. "How old would he be now?" He sifted through the letters and cards that were in the box until he found a little card from the funeral home that had both his mom's and dad's birth dates.

"October 1960 - 2009 and February 1958 - 2009. That makes him … That makes him fifty-seven, and Mom would be fifty-nine. Hey! She was older than dad." The more he thought about them, the more saddened he became.

He looked up at the clock. "Ten fifteen … What the heck?!"

He carelessly tossed the top back on the box of photos and pushed it across the table. He flagged his hand at the light switch on the way to his bedroom but missed it, not bothering to stop to make another attempt.

Saturday morning came too quickly. Tab sprang out of bed at five o'clock in the morning, his new standard wake-up time.

He wasn't picking up his grandpa for almost eight hours for the party, and he wasn't going in to work, so there wasn't any reason to get up so early, but he couldn't sleep.

Tab rifled through his dresser. Every time he found something suitable to wear there was a spot or a stain. Some of the clothes he found in his drawer were from high school, so they were out of the question.

In fact, his appearance hadn't been that important to him for years. Most of the time he wore the same clothes to work.

His grandfather had worn blue Dickies pants and shirts as long as he could remember. Tab followed his lead with the same blue Dickies shirts but with blue jeans. That just wasn't going to work for a birthday party. He also didn't want Willy seeing him look like such a bum.

He decided to give in and go to the store to find something worthy of the occasion. The only thing he had that wasn't old or out of date was the sport coat he bought for the auction, but he didn't need a long sleeve shirt and a jacket for a birthday party.

Tab started his day at the diner for breakfast. He had his pick of tables at six thirty on a Saturday morning. He sat in a corner booth as far away as possible from the one where he and Isabella used to sit.

Tab felt so conflicted every time he looked over at the empty booth. He and Isabella had such a great time together their senior year. He couldn't imagine the two of them ever being anything but best friends for the rest of his life. He found it more difficult every time he wrote her a letter. Why wasn't she writing back? What was he doing wrong? Six months of silence was almost too much to bear. Even Willy had drifted away. He served three nine-month tours in Iraq. Celeste and the kids kept him close to home. Every time Tab talked to him he was always on his way to do something with his kids.

Tab barely tasted his eggs and pancakes as his thoughts turned downward. In his life it seemed people left him little by little, until he was down to just one—his grandfather.

By the time he was finished, his mood was as bitter as his coffee. He couldn't take it anymore and decided to drive to the mall and wait in his car until it opened.

Once inside the mall, he saw a store he remembered when shopping with his mom. He thought if it was somewhere she would shop, then that's where he should go.

A short-sleeve polo shirt would be the right kind of shirt for the party, but after looking at the selection, he felt uncomfortable with all the bright colors. After nearly an hour of surveying every shirt in the store, he settled on a powder-blue button-down shirt. It was pale enough that it wouldn't draw too much attention, he hoped.

The less he had to interact with people he didn't know, the better. Tab had made a science of staying home and avoiding people. Hanging out at home was his specialty.

At half past seven, Tab pulled up to his grandpa's back door and gave two short honks of the horn.

When his grandfather came out, he tapped on the car window and leaned in as Tab rolled it down.

"Tab, can we take my car? My knees are giving me fits today. I'm afraid if I get in that little car, I'll never get out." Tab could see he wasn't joking, and he'd never asked before, so he knew it was important.

"Sure. I'll just pull around to the garage. Do you want me to drive?"

Benjamin nodded, "If you don't mind."

"Stay right here, and I'll be back in a minute."

Tab backed the car around the side of the house and pulled in front of the garage. He reappeared with his grandpa's old faded red Ford Taurus. Once his grandfather was in the car, they both looked at each other's unfamiliar dress for a long moment.

Tab had been expecting to see his grandfather in his usual blue pants and a white shirt and tie swapped out for his blue work shirt but was surprised to see a plaid short-sleeved shirt in its place. As for himself, he'd never worn a shirt the color of powder blue.

His grandfather spoke first. "Well, what do we have here? You're looking pretty dapper. Maybe there'll be—"

Tab stopped him midsentence. "You're killing me, Grandpa! Please, let's just go to the party."

"Okay, okay, but I think Willy's younger sister just graduated from college."

Tab rolled his eyes and shook his head as he threw the car in reverse. "You're killing me, Grandpa. You really are."

Tab thought nearly half of West Hartford was there when they walked through the door. He wasn't surprised that his grandpa knew almost everyone.

They were all crammed into a small room, waiting to explode with "Happy Birthday" when Willy's parents walked through the door.

Tab made his way around the entire room looking for Willy. To his surprise, he saw the familiar head of long, wavy black hair that could only be Isabella. His heart began to pound hard in his chest.

As he got closer, he saw Willy, then his little boy with his hands wrapped around … Isabella's leg. Tab stood on his toes to get a better look. It *was* Isabella, God she looked great!

He didn't know she had any plans to fly back for this party. She certainly hadn't thought to share her plans with him. He could hardly contain his excitement.

"Excuse me." Tab pressed his way through the crowd. He lost sight for a moment, and then he saw her holding the little boy. "Excuse me … Excuse me!" as he got closer, she had her back to him.

As he got closer, he reached out to touch her on the shoulder when he saw Willy put his arm around her. *Flash. Flash.* Several people took pictures of them.

He stopped in his tracks. It was Celeste! Tab's emotions went from excitement to feeling duped. Of course it was Celeste. What was he thinking?

He stood watching the two of them. He had no doubt they were having the time of their lives showing off the kids and saying hello to friends and family.

He couldn't take his eyes off her. She looked wonderful, not the provocatively dressed, overly made-up teenager he remembered. She was wearing a simple blue sleeveless dress with a pearl necklace. He'd always thought Isabella was prettier. He could only imagine what Isabella looked like now.

More and more people pressed their way around them trying to say hello. They both turned to greet someone behind them.

Celeste saw him first and excitedly called out to him, "Oh my God ... Tab!" She pulled him close. "Come over here! Willy, look who it is!" Willy's face lit up as he reached over his daughter and grabbed Tab around the neck.

Willy didn't let him go right away. "It's been so long. How are you doing?"

Tab was overcome by the feeling of loneliness. Before he knew it, he was wiping tears from his cheeks.

Celeste put her hands on Tab's shoulders and hugged him from behind, a gesture Tab wasn't expecting.

Celeste had made Isabella's teenage years difficult at times, but her kindness in that moment had a profound effect on Tab. He needed so badly to be with people he was once close to, just to talk, just to do nothing together. Tab could barely speak. Just as he started to say how much he missed them, the room erupted.

"Surprise!" everyone yelled in one loud chorus. Sounds of party horns and shouts of *happy birthday* filled the room. Willy's attention turned to his mother and father, who were just walking into the room.

"There they are!" he said to Celeste. He took each of his kids by the hand and took off for the front of the room with Celeste following close behind. Willy's mom greeted them with joy as she saw them pushing through the crowd. Tab could see the pure joy in Willy's parents as they gleefully embraced each other.

He truly felt happy for Willy and Celeste, getting to see Willy's parents after more than a year. Knowing nothing like that was ever going to happen for him, Tab pushing aside the pangs of jealousy and longing, making his way back to the table where his grandpa was sitting.

He screwed on a smile and told him that he got to see Willy for a few moments before Willy's parents came in.

His grandpa put his hand on Tab's forearm and said reassuringly, "I'm sure you'll get to spend more time with him. Let's go up and say hello to the Rosses. I'm sure they would love to see you."

They managed to get some face time with Willy's mom, her smile brightening when they exchanged greetings and hugs. "I see your grandfather all the time at church," Mrs. Ross said to Tab. "We would love to see you come again sometime."

"Thanks, Mrs. Ross. Maybe some time." Tab didn't really mean it, but it seemed to be the right thing to say.

Willy's father finished talking to another friend and turned to them. "Hey! My two favorite master craftsmen. Did you get a chance to see Willy yet?" Mr. Ross gave a quick scan of the room. "He's been busy saying hello to everyone. It's too bad they have to leave in the morning. They don't even have time to come to church with us tomorrow, but we'll take every second we can get with them. Did he tell you he was being transferred to Germany? They have to start packing as soon as they get home. Willy has to report for duty late next week."

Willy's dad could talk a mile a minute, but for Tab, it was slowly and painfully sinking in. He was so looking forward to seeing his old friend, and now he was leaving almost before he got here. He was mad at Willy for not leaving any time for the two of them to get together, and now Willy was moving to Germany.

Willy's mom was already talking to the next person in line. It was time to let the others give their happy birthday wishes. That was fine because Tab had heard about all he could take.

As they made their way back to the table, Tab could see that his grandpa was getting a little tired from all the walking and standing. It was the perfect excuse for Tab to leave early, even though he would feel guilty doing so.

"Are you okay, Tab? I can see you're upset."

"No … I'm not upset. I'm fine, just fine."

"I'm sure it was a surprise to hear about Willy and Celeste moving to Germany."

Tab screwed on a smile again. "I'm happy for them. It sounds like a great adventure." He worked hard to hide his emotions from his grandpa, but he knew his grandpa could almost always see straight through him.

The two of them sat mostly alone at the corner table. Tab got them both a generous helping of birthday cake. Patiently, they sat through Willy's father making a speech about how lucky he was to have so many wonderful friends take off a beautiful Saturday afternoon to come share his birthday cake with him.

Willy's mom announced they were going on an Alaskan cruise in a few weeks. Then Willy made a toast to the two most wonderful parents a man could ever have.

All the while, Tab was on a roller coaster of emotions that made him feel sick to his stomach, and he couldn't wait to get off.

His grandfather was finally ready to go. Tab wanted to slip away without anyone noticing. "I'll go get the car. I'll see you at the door." Then he zoomed down the hallway.

His grandpa wasn't at the door when he pulled up in the Taurus, so he waited for several minutes.

Twenty minutes went by when he decided to go in and see if his grandfather was okay.

As Tab stepped on the curb, he saw his grandpa and Willy at the door. "Hey, what's going on? Trying to sneak out without saying goodbye?" Willy asked.

"I'm sorry. Grandpa needed to head home, and you were surrounded by so many of your parents' friends that I didn't want to get in the way."

"Are you kidding? Everyone knows we were buds."

Tab opened the door for his grandpa to keep their exit moving along. "Can I help you, Grandpa?"

"No, Tab. I'm all right." He grimaced as he lowered himself into the passenger seat. Tab carefully closed his door and turned to Willy.

"Well, I guess this is goodbye. Your dad said you leave in the morning for Germany."

"I'm sorry, Tab. We just couldn't get any more time away. This assignment is a great opportunity for us. After a few years, I'll have the chance to move back and become an instructor so I won't have to fly as much. I'll be home every night."

Willy wrapped his arms around his oldest and dearest friend. "It's good to see you."

"Yeah, it's good to see you too. Germany … That's pretty far way."

Tab slipped into the driver's seat and started the car. He bent down to see Willy's face through the passenger's side window and waved to his old friend as he shifted into drive.

Willy took a few steps along with the car as they started to pull away. Then he slapped his hand on the roof and yelled, "Hang on, hang on."

Tab stopped the car abruptly.

Willy bent down to the passenger's side window. "Meet me in the park at seven. I'll be at the picnic table waiting for you. There's something we need to talk about."

Tab nodded with a smile as Willy ran back to the party.

Seven o'clock felt pretty lonely as Tab sat by himself waiting for Willy. Across the park, Tab watched people come and go—a young couple tossing a Frisbee, another standing on either side of the swing gently pushing their giggling baby.

Almost an hour had gone by when he saw Willy and Celeste herding their kids across the park toward the swing set. Celeste got them situated so she could push one and then the other. Then Willy joined him at the picnic table.

"Hey, Willy, thanks for taking the time to come and see me. I know you want to spend time with your mom and dad."

"The kids were bouncing off the walls anyway. We needed to get them outside to use up their last bit of energy."

"Well, anyway ... thanks."

Willy watched his kids swing for a few moments while Tab looked at the rough, aged wood of the picnic table. A lot had happened in this very spot. They skateboarded here every summer. They fantasized about the life his Uncle Ronny led and how fantastic it would be to see the world. And this was where Willy told him he was going to marry Celeste. They had gotten pregnant, so Willy did the honorable thing by marrying Celeste, and then he enlisted in the army.

Tab followed Willy's gaze, seeing the happy, smiling children, and thought things turned out well for his old friend.

"You know how many times we've sat here at this picnic table?" asked Tab.

"Yeah, we made some big decisions sitting right here." Willy gave him a knowing look, and Tab knew he remembered too.

"You know, Celeste and I … We didn't get started out the best way, but I have the life of my dreams. I have a great job, and Celeste is a great mom to Billy and Chloe. My little peanuts are the loves of my life. I just can't tell you how happy I am."

"Yeah, they look great! I can tell Celeste is really good with them."

Willy nodded but seemed to have more on his mind. "Tab, I don't know any other way to say this, but Celeste and I … well … We're worried about you."

"I'm doing just fine."

"You're still moping around."

"I'm not moping. I'm keeping busy. I've been putting so many hours in at the shop I just don't have time for anything else."

"Come on, Tab. That's a cop-out. I know you better than you know yourself. When I'm not here to drag you out, you close yourself off. Life is more than work all day and video games and microwave hot dogs by night."

Tab hopped off the table and scowled at Willy. "Easy for you to say. Every time I get close to someone, they leave. My grandma, mom and dad, you, Isabella, I just can't do it anymore."

Willy's shoulders were relaxed, and he looked at Tab calmly. "Have you ever flown on a plane with a back door big enough to drive a truck through at five thousand feet?"

Tab didn't know where Willy was going with this, but he listened.

"We open it up and push huge palettes of supplies out to parachute to the ground. It's not a very safe thing to do. There are a lot of ways to die in my job, but I know the risks, and I'm damn good at what I do."

"I get it. Things can go wrong in your line of work."

Willy fully faced him. "I'm just as likely to lose my family by some idiot texting and driving, killing Celeste and the kids."

That cold reality settled over Tab. He hung his head as he kicked at the ground and searched for the right words to defend his isolation.

"There are risks in living life … but there are great rewards too," Willy continued.

"Maybe for you. I lost my parents suddenly and horribly. It changed everything."

"I know … I'm not saying it shouldn't, but life is passing you by." Willy looked at him and sighed. "Let me tell you a story."

102

"Okay." Tab sat down again.

"A man searches the world to find the meaning of life. He finally reaches the top of a mountain and asks the wise man, 'What is the meaning of life?' The wise man replies, 'The grandfather dies, the father dies, and the son dies.' The man replies, 'That's horrible.' The wise man says, 'Would you have it any other way?'"

Tab wasn't sure he liked this story. "It didn't work out like that for me."

"You're missing the point. The grandfather had a son, and the son had a son."

The answer felt just out of Tab's reach.

Willy looked at him plainly. "Life goes on with you or without you."

Celeste called to them. "Hey, honey. We've got to go."

They turned to see the kids looking tired, and Billy was squirming in Celeste's arms.

"Okay, I'm coming." Willy slid off the table. "Think about what I said."

Tab nodded that he would simply because he didn't want to talk about it anymore.

Willy lifted Chloe on his shoulders, and they all made their way over to the car and buckled the exhausted kids in their seats. They took turns giving Tab hugs goodbye and reluctantly left him in the parking lot alone.

Tab waved with a smile until they drove off around the corner, his smile draining quickly from his face as they disappeared from sight.

Tab drove back to his apartment, retreating to his place of safety. He had been so looking forward to this day, but now he was more than ready for it to be over.

As soon as he entered the lobby, Tab checked his mailbox. *Please let there be something from Isabella.* He needed something good to make up for all the bad. But still, no letter. He tried to make peace with his disappointment, but it was harder this time.

In a few minutes, he was in his gym shorts and an old T-shirt and in his chair in front of the television, ready for another night of channel surfing.

As he clicked through the channels, Willy's words kept gnawing at him. Was life passing him by?

Tab never told his grandfather that when he was in high school, he had talked to Uncle Ronny about enlisting. It didn't matter because in the end he had stayed behind.

In any case, he had become a fine craftsman in his own right. Since he grew up in the shop, he had many more years of experience than others his age. He had decided to continue working with his grandfather. His grandfather constantly challenged him, and Tab was always up to the task.

But it just wasn't enough. He wondered what his life would have been like if he had joined the Army with Willy, or maybe followed Isabella to Spokane for college.

Tab was sure Isabella was coming home—she had to, at least that's what he'd been telling himself. He thought about how her letters got further and further apart.

Tab racked his brain trying to figure out what went wrong.

He knew she valued her freedom, so at first, he didn't think anything of it.

In high school, Tab was honored when she brought over her catalogs for the colleges she was applying to.

He had asked her, "Why are you looking at schools so far away?"

At first, Isabella didn't answer, but then she said, "I want to get as far away from home as possible." Tab felt a little sad that they weren't going to be able to see each other all the time, but reluctantly, he understood.

School became her singular focus, spending her time studying and at night waiting tables at a local restaurant. She told him many times she was determined not to let anything get in the way of completing her goal. She had promised never to be in a position where she had to depend on anyone else to put a roof over her head.

Throughout college, Isabella never made any visits back to West Hartford. She attended a job fair prior to graduation and discovered the city of Macau, China, was looking for an English teacher.

Macau was becoming one of the largest gambling cities in the world. They wanted more of their casino and restaurant workers to speak English. It didn't take long for her to make the decision to go.

Tab remembered how excited she sounded when she spoke of

working in Macau. In three years, she would be able to pay off most of her school loans.

He had high hopes she would come home afterward, but now he wasn't sure she would ever come back.

He took the big stack of letters off his desk and sat reading through each one, trying to see if he could get some kind of clue for her extended silences, checking to make sure he hadn't written anything that made her stop.

When Isabella wrote more frequently, she told him all about her studies and sent an occasional photo. His grandfather had kept one in particular hanging in his grandmother's room. It was Isabella at a beach sitting on a big rock with the ocean in the background.

Tab couldn't find any hint that she was unhappy with him.

He sat thinking about what he was going to do. He couldn't wait forever. Maybe Willy was right. Maybe it was time to let her go.

Tab took the letters and neatly placed them next to his dusty old books on the top of his bookshelf—a place where he kept things that he would never read again.

Chapter 8

Ellen's Room

TAB HAD FINISHED THE HUGE job of preparing the cherry boards and was well under way with his challenge. Over the last few weeks, he had carved the elegant Queen Anne legs and assembled the lower half of the highboy. As he finished the upper section, it marked the halfway point of the project.

Tab enjoyed the little notes old Tabner had made on his original drawings, faded and barely visible 150 years since they were first drawn. The little comments in the margin were important clues about how old Tabner was and his ideas as he was creating and refining his masterpiece.

Tab didn't feel right about making his own notes directly on the plans, so he placed sticky notes on the drawings instead.

Tab had made many drawers, but this set would be different. For years, the shop had used poplar, a common and plentiful material for the drawer sides and bottoms, but the highboy would have white pine, which was the common wood for most Connecticut furniture of the 1850s. These two woods are very different to work with. Poplar is a soft wood that is very easy to carve, while the white pine is also soft but has an added feature of winter and summer grain that gives the drawers their ribbed look and makes it harder to work with a chisel.

Tab had decided to make a sample drawer to practice working with the pine. By the end of the test drawer, the differences were clear, and he was confident he could make the drawers.

He wanted to start with the three bottom drawers that were equal in size. The center drawer had the fan motif cut deeply into its face. Tab would have to carve the drawer face before he built the drawer.

Tab spent hours in the evening studying old Tabner's fan design and drawing several fans of his own to show his grandfather. After a long discussion about how the lines of the shape flowed, how one area needed to balance with the other, his grandfather encouraged Tab to make a few changes and make it his own.

Now that he was confident of his design, he began marking out the fan and choosing the chisels and gouges he would need to bring his design to life.

When Tab was younger, he remembered his father describing his process of carving and being able to see the finished piece in his head while he worked. As Tab carved, he had the same sensation. He removed the bulk of the wood quickly but carefully. Then he focused on making the refined cuts to the finished carving.

He could feel his grandfather keeping a close eye on his work, as if trying hard not to give advice but offering as much encouragement as he could. "Nice job carving the fan, Tab—very nice design!"

Tab could tell he even seemed impressed with the quality of the work, which only improved Tab's confidence.

The phone rang, and his grandfather answered with his usual pleasant greeting as he had for more than fifty years. "Hello, Kirkman's. How can I help you? Oh, hello, Phil."

After they exchanged pleasantries, his grandfather's face grew serious. "Sure, Phil. Is there a problem?"

Tab put down his carving tools while his grandfather listened to Mr. Scott on the line.

After a few moments, his grandfather said, "I would be happy to do what I can. Okay, Phil, I'll let you know when we see it."

He said goodbye and hung up the phone. Then he turned to Tab.

"What's going on, Grandpa?"

"The highboy that was sold to Mr. Campbell has been damaged by Clement's movers."

The following morning, both Benjamin and Tab were in the shop early even though Tab wasn't working on his highboy. They were anxious to hear from Phil again, or Mr. Campbell, about seeing the damaged highboy and how they could help with the repairs. Clement's was taking full responsibility.

The phone rang as the minute hand on Benjamin's clock reached nine o'clock. He answered the phone on the first ring.

The voice at the other end of the line said, "Hello, this is Robert Campbell. I'm calling about the Kirkman highboy."

Benjamin said, "Yes, of course, Mr. Campbell. We've been expecting your call."

"Mr. Kirkman, I can't tell you how sick I am that this has happened. I take my stewardship of the things entrusted to my care very seriously. I sure hope you can help make this treasure whole again."

They would do their best to restore the old piece back to its original condition. After a description of the damage, Benjamin assured him that it could be done.

They made arrangements for Benjamin and Tab to come out the following week to Mr. Campbell's home to take a look at the highboy.

After the morning's work, Tab said, "I'll make some sandwiches for lunch."

"You just want to avoid the goose liver. All right. Let's see what you can come up with. I'm going to go check the mail."

Benjamin walked out to the front porch and down the rough stone driveway.

It had been a very fulfilling month for Benjamin, watching Tab lay out the curved front sections, carve the decorative crown, and work out the difficult structure of the moldings. It put a smile on his face. Benjamin was feeling good about his decision to have Tab take on this huge project.

On his way back to the house, he thumbed through the junk mail and the bills and came across an unexpected letter.

The return address was Macau, China, and it was addressed to both of them. Benjamin walked to the kitchen where Tab had peanut butter and pickle sandwiches on the table with a cup of coffee for Benjamin and a Coke for himself.

Benjamin sat down and slid the letter from China across the table toward Tab.

Tab looked down at the address and said, "Oh my God. It's been almost nine months since we've heard from her!"

When Tab hesitated, Benjamin said, "Go ahead, open it."

Tab tore the envelope open and unfolded the letter. After a moment, he handed the letter to Benjamin.

There were only three sentences on the page:

> *Dear Friends,*
>
> *I'm tired, and it's time to come home. I will be arriving at the Newark airport at 5 o'clock on September 3. Can you give me a ride back to West Hartford?*
>
> *Your friend,*
> *Isabella*

Tab hopped off his chair like he was sitting on a spring and rushed over to look at the calendar, the one Benjamin's auto insurance agent sent every year.

"One, two, three, four weeks. Do you think she'll get a letter before she leaves if we send it out today?"

"Oh, I'm sure she will, but let's make sure we get it out today."

Tab inhaled his lunch, rushing to clear the plates before Benjamin was even finished with his last two bites. Tab reached for his grandfather's coffee mug. Putting his hand over it, Benjamin barked, "No, I'm not done! We'll get to the shop in plenty of time to get your letter out."

Tab sat back in his seat, his leg bouncing impatiently, while Benjamin finished his coffee.

Eventually, Benjamin stood and carried his mug to the sink. He grinned over his shoulder at Tab, "Well, what are you waiting for, time's a wasting!"

Tab hesitated, slowing his steps to match Benjamin's on their short commute to the shop. He reached forward to hold the door for him as they entered.

Tab went straight to Benjamin's desk to write out his reply to Isabella. With pen in hand, Tab looked down at the blank sheet of paper but didn't write a thing. He turned to Benjamin, "It's been a while … What do you think I should say?"

In a soft voice, his grandfather replied, "Keep it short … She did."

He looked back down again at the paper, searching for the right words. He tossed his pen back into the jar and grabbed a big black magic marker and wrote: *YES!*

No signature needed, Tab stuck it in an envelope and wrote down Isabella's address.

"I'm going to take it to the post office to make sure it goes out today." He flung open the door so hard that it made a loud sound as it slammed against the shop wall. He yelled a loud, "Sorry!" as he trotted toward his car.

Benjamin grinned and shook his head as he heard Tab's tires squeal when his car turned on to the street. He knew Tab was excited about Isabella's return, and he was happy that she was coming back to West Hartford, but he had serious concerns about how her return was going to affect Tab. Was she going to stay in New Hartford or move on and leave Tab behind again? One thing was for sure, like his aging knees, he had absolutely no control over the outcome.

After about twenty minutes, Tab returned to the shop and went back to his bench. Benjamin watched him as he tied on his apron and picked up his plane to continue flattening the boards for the drawer bottoms when Benjamin said, "You did put stamps on that letter, didn't you?"

Tab stopped mid-motion and hung his head, untied his apron, and walked back over to the desk to rewrite his letter.

After his second try, Tab was able to get back to flattening his drawer bottoms.

Tab thought back to the last time he had seen Isabella.

After high school graduation, Tab was surprised to hear that Isabella was moving to Spokane, Washington, for college. She told Tab that it was because she found a job and had to get there quickly so she didn't lose it, but Tab suspected the real reason was her unbearable homelife. Even Celeste had already moved out.

Tab was heartbroken that she was leaving so soon. He tried to spend as much time with her as he could before she left. Their friendship started with their platonic arrangement, but she had become a real friend and confidant.

The two of them spent lots of time together, and Isabella was a frequent guest at the Kirkmans' dinner table. Isabella even waved some of her restrictions, holding hands and even dancing, so that they wouldn't look too strange at the senior prom. The old hotel ballroom and usual prom costumes made their charade complete. However, the rules returned as soon as the prom ended. Neither of them wanted to go to any of the late-night parties; instead, they spent the last hours of the night with his grandfather.

As Isabella's departure date came, a huge veil of dread weighed on him. He arranged to take her out for breakfast at their favorite diner and sit in their special booth. For Tab, it would always be *their booth*.

They sat and reminisced about the year they had together. Tab wanted the moment to last forever, but the time flew by so quickly, and before he knew it, it was time to go. Tab drove her to the workshop so she could say goodbye to his grandfather.

He waited in the car to give them their tearful moment together. Isabella and his grandfather had formed a close friendship too. They were like family.

Isabella walked back to the car and tried to hide her tears as she buckled herself in. Tab reluctantly started the car and slowly set off toward the airport.

The drive seemed far too short as Tab drove up the departure ramp. He had plenty of things to say but couldn't get a single one of them out.

Tab stopped the car under the airline's sign and pulled the lever that opened the trunk. They both got out, knowing their time was up. Tab lifted her overstuffed bags out of the trunk and onto the curb. *This was it*, Tab thought.

They stood face-to-face.

Tab finally said, "I'm breaking one of your rules," as he bent down and kissed her on both cheeks. "I owed you those for almost a year."

Isabella wrapped her arms around him and said, "You're the best friend I've ever had," and squeezed him a little tighter.

"I've wanted to say something to you all day, but I just couldn't get the words out." They gently released each other, and he took a deep breath. "I know how badly you need to leave, but if you ever wonder where home is, I hope West Hartford is somewhere to come home to."

Fresh tears filled Isabella's eyes as she gave him another big hug. Then, unable to meet his eyes again, she spun her suitcase around and ran to the door.

The airport security guard had made his way down to Tab's car by then, and he knew he had to go.

The drive back home left him alone with his thoughts and sorrow.

He hoped this wasn't the end of Isabella in his life. His friends were all gone, and he didn't think he could bear the risk of starting another friendship and losing it too.

Tab dragged himself back to the shop, entered quietly, sat on his stool, and heaved a heavy sigh. The morning was his lowest since he had lost his parents. "Well, Grandpa, she's gone."

His grandfather was sitting at his bench sifting through some paperwork without really looking at it. As soon as Tab returned, he tossed it aside and faced him. "I know, Tab. It doesn't feel very good, does it?"

"I feel like I've been kicked in the gut."

"Tab, you may not know it, but you've experienced your first love. You've been given a great gift."

He hung his head. "We're just friends."

His grandfather continued. "Your love didn't start like the love of most young men with the physical attraction and the lust that comes along with it. It came from respect and acceptance, to have someone who could listen and understand and not judge. Tab, I've never been as proud of anyone as I have been of you this past year."

"Grandpa, I think I've made a horrible mistake. I should have stopped her. I should have asked her to stay."

"But, Tab, don't you understand? You've given her the greatest gift of all. She needed to go and get away from her life here, and you gave her the opportunity to find her own way."

"Grandpa, do you think she'll ever come back?" he said, looking into his grandfather's kind eyes.

"I don't think we've seen the last of our Isabella."

Chapter 9

❧❦

Restoration

T HE KIRKMAN SHOP WAS BUSY all week with Tab's highboy and other commissions. They went through their usual weekend routine with lunch at the diner and Benjamin asking Tab if he wanted to go to church. Monday, they drove into Rye, New York, to see Mr. Campbell.

Tab had never been to Rye, and he could only imagine what Mr. Campbell's house was like. Someone with the kind of money he had, spending hundreds of thousands of dollars on an old dresser and having his own limo and driver, must live in some kind of palace.

Tab volunteered to drive them in his car. He was starting to feel self-conscious riding around in his grandfather's car, but he remembered his grandfather had difficulty getting in and out of the sporty low seats of his Mustang. So, he grabbed the keys for the faded old rocket ship.

Tab struggled to see the addresses as they drove past well-manicured hedges.

Finally, his grandfather said, "This is it, right here!"

Tab slowly pulled up to a huge gate. "Now what do we do?"

Again, his grandfather pointed to the call box on the post near the driver's side door. "Try pushing one of those buttons."

Tab lowered the window, and as he reached for the button, he heard a familiar voice say, "Hello, please come on in."

The huge gate swung open. Tab put the car in drive with a grin. "Wow, I feel like I'm in some kind of Hollywood movie."

His grandfather laughed and said, "I know what you mean."

The tires made a crackling sound as they rolled over the cobblestone drive that led under a brick archway. They both leaned forward to see what was on the other side. As they drove out from under the archway and into the daylight, the huge mansion came into view.

"Now, I know we're in a movie! Good grief, look at that thing," Tab said, as he followed the drive around a fountain and up to the front door. "I feel a little like I'm the help, and I'm driving up to the wrong door."

His grandfather said, "Well, this is a first for me. I feel just a little underdressed."

Tab thought about how improbable it was to have been invited to visit a house like this. They were both in awe of the home's majesty. Neither one of them noticed the massive front door open.

"Hello, gentlemen," Mr. Campbell said. "I'm so thankful you were able to come out today. I've been looking forward to having you visit since the auction."

They exchanged pleasantries as he invited them into the spacious two-story foyer.

Totally stunned by the opulence of the home, Tab tried his best not to let his jaw hang open.

His grandfather also looked mesmerized with what he saw. "You have a beautiful home, Mr. Campbell."

"Please, call me Robert. Thank you. My wife and I have enjoyed restoring it and, of course, filling it with interesting things." He pointed them toward a large study with incredible paintings, furniture, and all kinds of glass and bronze artwork.

Tab could hear his mom's voice in his head, "Keep your hands in your pockets, and don't touch anything!"

Robert showed them room after room, each as beautiful as the one before. At last he took them up the steps to one of the bedrooms. They were both surprised to see a room filled with Kirkman furniture.

"Please, look around. I'm interested to hear what you think of these pieces."

His grandfather walked around the room, looking at each of their family's creations.

Tab thought about all the fabulous and exotic things he had seen in the Campbells' house, some of them worth hundreds of thousands of dollars, and now a room full of Kirkman furniture. How was it possible that his family could be that interesting to someone who owned so many valuable possessions?

"Mr. Cam—Robert."

"Yes, Tab."

"Can I ask you about your collection?"

"Of course."

"You have all these amazing things. Why would you want all this Kirkman furniture?"

"That's a very good question. We have traveled around the world looking for treasures. The most important thing about collecting is to collect only what you like, and we like Kirkman furniture."

His grandfather pointed at a low vanity. "This was made by my father and grandfather. They only made a few of these. My grandmother had one of them."

"Only a few? I had no idea. That makes it even more special."

His grandfather pointed to the bed. "This is really something ... Tab, look at that wood. Can you imagine working with that?"

"I bought this set at an antique store in Ohio when I was on a business trip. The bed had already been converted to a modern mattress size, but thankfully, they didn't damage the original side boards."

Tab ran his hands over the footboard with a heart motif cut through the richly colored wood. He felt the intense ripples of the boldly flamed maple. "Wow, that's amazing wood—what a beautiful color."

"This was probably made by Floyd," Benjamin said as he thought back to the listings in his small book. "We could look for numbers to make sure, but first we should probably look at the highboy and see how badly it's damaged."

"Yes, please. This is really an embarrassment to have this happen."

The threesome gathered around the highboy across the room, and Robert recounted what had happened.

The two movers had removed all the drawers and stacked them at the top of the steps on top of a moving blanket. Then they carried the body of the highboy up and brought it into the room, after which they came out to get each drawer. When one of the movers reached down to pick up the last drawer, the other grabbed the moving blanket underneath, and that's where it got a little dicey. The drawer tumbled down the steps, bouncing and crashing on its way. By the time it came to rest at the bottom, it was in pieces.

Robert pointing, "It's the top drawer with the beautiful fan carving."

"Well, it doesn't look too badly damaged from here." His grandfather reached up to pull it out. As he did, the drawer front came away without the rest of the drawer. "Oh, I see. A little glue won't do—nope, won't do at all."

Robert said, "I was afraid of that."

His grandfather looked over the drawer front. "I'm surprised that it's almost completely untouched, but ..."

As he examined the rest, he shared a knowing look with Tab. It was completely destroyed.

"I think the best thing to do is to bring the whole thing to our shop so we can rebuild the drawer. I'll use my movers this time just to be safe."

"Then we'll make the arrangements. I'm so glad you can make it right."

Robert continued the house tour after hearing the good news about the highboy. They spent nearly three hours enjoying the treasures the Campbells had collected over the years.

Tab thought it was a little bit like a museum, and it still felt a little weird that he collected all that Kirkman furniture. With old Tabner's highboy coming home, how could all these circumstances come together? Making his own highboy at the same time the old dresser was going to be in the shop was going to be a real treat.

A week had gone by before the highboy arrived. Tab had rearranged the shop to make room. For Benjamin, it was a magical moment—two highboys separated by more than 150 years, also made by a Kirkman named Tabner.

They both sat on the bench across the room and observed them, each pointing at different parts and comparing the work.

Tab's highboy was still missing the drawers and the finials, but Benjamin could see the maturity of Tab's work.

"I may never have such a fine Kirkman piece in the shop as an example again. I'm looking forward to having it here for the next few weeks," as Tab continues to study the old highboy.

Benjamin knew it would take about two or three months to complete the drawers because of Tab's limited work schedule, but he was sure Tab would make steady progress soon enough. He started at the bottom, and worked his way up the center drawer to the raised sea-fan carving.

Old Tabner's highboy would be long gone before Tab was finished, but Benjamin agreed it was great to have it in the shop for inspiration.

Benjamin wanted to find the best wood for his repair, matching the drawer's original pine. He and Tab spent a good part of a morning scrounging around the woodshed for just the right piece. Benjamin kept all kinds of odd pieces of wood just for this purpose.

Tab had never done any repairs like this, so Benjamin made sure Tab saw how he was going to do it. Once they had chosen the pine, Benjamin planed it down close to finish size.

He told Tab that he wanted to give the replacement wood time to stabilize before he started to fit everything together.

Benjamin was glad Mr. Campbell was willing to give him plenty of time to do the repair, even though it would take just a few weeks. He wanted to take advantage of his interest in visiting the shop so that he could show off his young apprentice's work.

They had planned his visit for the Saturday before Isabella's return.

Mr. Campbell arrived mid-morning accompanied by his wife.

Benjamin and Tab met them in the driveway. "Welcome," said Benjamin.

"Gentlemen, it's good to see you again. I'd like you to meet my wife, Connie."

They exchanged greetings. "Robert has told me so much about the both of you. I'm so pleased that we were able to visit your workshop."

As they entered the shop, Benjamin explained the odd layout of the workshop. As he did with most of his guests, he explained how it optimized the use of daylight.

They stopped in front of the two highboys standing side by side.

"This one is Tab's." Benjamin explained Tab's challenge with the added difficulty of making it with only hand tools.

Tab was eager to show off his work and invited them to take a closer look.

They listened intently as Tab explained his challenge. Benjamin was pleasantly surprised at how confidently Tab talked to them.

Tab had finished four of the nine drawers, and the beauty of his wood selection was starting to give the highboy a character of its own.

Mr. Campbell turned to Tab. "Did you really do all this work without any power tools?"

"Yes, sir! I even used an old treadle-powered grinding wheel to sharpen my tools. Grandpa won't even let me turn on the lights. That's pretty hard on a rainy day."

"Young man, I have looked at hundreds of pieces of furniture, old and new, and I can tell you in all honesty, I've not seen better work. Even this beautiful piece standing next to it doesn't compare."

Tab's mouth hung open in surprise.

Mrs. Campbell gave a small laugh. "I think you shocked him, Robert."

Benjamin said, "Yes, thank you, Robert, for those kind words. I think you took his breath away." Benjamin patted Tab on the back.

Tab smiled and reached out to shake his hand and said, "Thank you, thank you. I've only had my grandfather's comments up until now, and you know … well … He *is* my grandpa."

"I'm looking forward to seeing it when you have completed it. That beautiful wood is going to look fantastic when it's varnished."

Benjamin was pleased. The highboy gave Tab the confidence and passion he needed to continue, but recognition was powerful for a craftsman too. It was validation.

Having the Campbells visit was a wonderful gift for both of them.

Benjamin said, "Before you go, I would love to show you my little Kirkman collection. I've managed to keep a few things along the way that I think are pretty special."

"Nothing would please us more than to see your lovely things. It's always a treat to see what others find important to collect."

The Campbells followed as Benjamin made his way up to the house.

"Looks like those old knees of yours are complaining again today." Mr. Campbell reached out his hand to help him up the steps.

"Well, thanks for the concern. Standing in one place really does get to them sometimes. I'll be okay in a bit." Out of respect for his new friend, he accepted his offer of help.

The Campbells followed him into his living room, which was overflowing with old family pieces. Many of them were pieces Tab's mother had collected.

He pointed out a corner shelf that was covered with pierced carvings. It made the piece airy and light in appearance. "My grandfather made it for his wife as a fortieth anniversary gift. It's covered with dogwood blossoms, her favorite flower. It's a one of a kind, like some of the other things in here."

Connie said, "The lamp on the corner table with the wood and stained glass with the oak frame ... We've seen lamps like it before. How can we tell if it was from your family's shop?"

Benjamin stood with one hand on his hip and shook his head with a soft nod and then looked up with a smile and said, "I don't believe you can. They're probably from the '20s or '30s. This one doesn't have any numbers like a lot of the small things they made. Tab's mom had a real knack for figuring out these old things."

He showed them into Ellen's room and pointed to the little desk. "My father made this desk for his sister, Lilly. She was only four foot six. He thought she was a very special person. He and my mother loved making special things for her."

They spent the rest of the morning looking at the treasures in Benjamin's home, and when the Campbells offered to take them out to lunch, Benjamin graciously accepted and told them about his favorite diner.

They spent a leisurely two hours talking over lunch.

Benjamin agreed to come back to their house to look at the other Kirkman pieces to see if he could put dates on them like he had with the highboy.

By the end of lunch, Benjamin and the Campbells had become best of friends.

While driving back to the shop, Benjamin said to Tab, "Let's call it a day. I'm ready to put my feet up."

"Fine by me. I have to clean my apartment anyway."

Benjamin grinned but said nothing. He had a feeling this had something to do with Isabella coming home soon.

As the third of September grew closer, Tab could barely keep his mind on his work. He was running all kinds of scenarios through his head regarding Isabella.

Since her absence, many of Tab's short-lived relationships had ended when he avoided romance. But he hoped he and Isabella could continue their arrangement like they had when they were in high school.

He had been so lonely since she left.

Soon the day would arrive when it was time to bring her home.

Tab and his grandfather set off for the airport with plenty of extra time to make sure they wouldn't be late. They decided to park the car and enter the airport to wait for her.

Tab watched for the arrivals on the television screens looking for her flight from Hong Kong. They were surprised to see it had arrived almost twenty minutes early, but they knew she would have to go through customs, and that would take some time.

Standing outside the restricted area, Tab strained to catch a glimpse of Isabella, scanning every face as people walked by.

Then Tab saw a familiar head of black hair among the crowd. He swallowed hard. Even though he was nearly as tall as his grandfather, he jumped in the air to get a better look. His heart was pounding in anticipation as he turned to his grandfather. "I think I see her!"

As she came closer, he was sure it was her and pointed her out to his grandfather at the same time she laid eyes on them.

Isabella's face lit up as she weaved her way through the crowd. "Oh my God. I've missed you both so much!" She gave his grandfather a big hug.

Tab was a little disappointed that he didn't receive her first hug, but as quickly as he had his thoughts, she reached out for him and wrapped her arms around him tightly.

After a long moment, she stepped back and then planted a big kiss on each cheek and said, "There. I owed you that!" She stepped back as she wiped away her tears.

Tab could barely believe he was looking at his old friend after so long. He thought she was exactly the same at first, but the more he looked, the more he realized she wasn't the same person who left West Hartford nearly seven years ago.

Isabella dropped her backpack on the ground and pushed her long black hair back over her shoulders, stopping mid-motion. "What?" She exclaimed, grinning from ear to ear.

"You're a sight for sore eyes ... I mean, you look good ... I mean ..." Tab had turned two shades of red in his embarrassment.

Isabella laughed and said, "You're a sight for sore eyes yourself." She picked up her backpack and threw it back over her shoulder.

Benjamin smiled as he watched the two of them exchange grins and glances.

She grabbed them each by the arm and said, "Let's get out of here."

Tab pointed at the luggage sign. "This way ..."

"This is all the luggage I have."

His grandfather looked at her single bag. "That's all?"

"The school sent all my stuff by freight for me. I had them send it to your house. I hope you don't mind."

Tab placed her bag in the trunk and opened the front passenger door for her, but she insisted his grandfather sit in front out of respect.

"I've been traveling for almost twenty-four hours. I'm not sure I can stay awake until we get back to West Hartford." She slid into the back seat and buckled herself in.

Tab wished Isabella had sat next to him, but of course his grandfather needed to sit in the front seat because of his knees. The trip home went quickly, and in no time, they pulled into the driveway.

Isabella had fallen fast asleep in the back seat only to be awakened as the car came to an abrupt stop in front of the garage.

Benjamin carried her bag up to the house while Tab opened her door. She wrapped her arm around Tab's as they walked toward the house. This was clearly a violation of their rules, but he wasn't going to complain—at least not tonight.

"Can I get you anything to eat or drink? Do you need anything?" asked Benjamin.

Isabella sat down at the kitchen table for a moment. She slid her hands out and back across the table and said, "I have a lot of fond memories of the three of us around this table. The year I spent hanging out here with the two of you was truly special."

It was nearly ten o'clock when Benjamin urged her to go get herself settled in Ellen's room. Looking at her watch, Isabella agreed it was late.

Benjamin said, "You know this old house as well as anyone, so just make yourself at home, and we'll have plenty of time tomorrow to catch up."

She gave them both hugs again and pushed them out the door, closing it behind them. "We'll talk in the morning, boys!"

Chapter 10

❧

Reconciliation

BENJAMIN WAS MAKING HIS MORNING coffee when he was startled, seeing his wife's robe walk in the room after so many years.

It was Isabella, wearing one of the few clothing items he'd left available to her in Ellen's small closet.

"Isabella! I didn't expect to see you so early in the morning."

"I've been up since five o'clock because of my jetlag. I didn't want to wake you, but then I heard you come down the stairs." She pointed to the clock. "It's almost dinner time for me back in Macau."

"Oh, I never thought about that. I could make you dinner if you like."

"No thank you, but I would love some coffee. The smell of it made it impossible to stay in bed."

He took a mug from the cabinet and poured a generous portion.

As he handed her the mug, tears started to well up in her eyes. She looked up at Benjamin as she pulled free the key that hung around her neck that he had given to her several years earlier.

"The day you gave this to me, I knew I could make it through the next year of school because I had options. Now … I need to use this for a while. I have nowhere else to go."

Benjamin was a little choked up himself. "Oh, sweetie, I wouldn't have it any other way." He leaned in to give her a hug and said, "I'm so glad you're finally home.

"Thank you so much … for everything … Without you and Tab,

123

I wouldn't have anywhere to call home. You know, they say home is where the heart is. I know it's a cliché, but it's true."

Benjamin knew Isabella had a stormy relationship with her mother. It was apparent that her time away had changed her. He hoped he could tell her about her mother—but not just yet.

"I'm honored this was where you wanted to come home to. I want you to consider this home for as long as you would like. I know Tab would like to have you close by too."

He knew Tab had shut himself off from any relationship because of his loss, but he hoped both Tab and Isabella could heal from their wounds and find some joy in life. They had a deep connection even though they had spent years apart. When they were together, their relationship had the appearance of a brother-sister companionship, but Benjamin hoped someday it would become much more.

Isabella reached out and placed her hand on his, "You overwhelm me. Thank you so much."

"My Ellen would be so happy to have you here. I wish the two of you could have met. You would have been fast friends, I'm sure."

Benjamin got up from the table and placed his plate in the sink. "I'm late for work. I better get moving, or Tab will be in before I am."

"You go ahead. I'll take care of your dishes."

"Thank you, sweetie," Benjamin said as he poured himself another cup of coffee and headed for the shop.

Tab arrived shortly after Benjamin opened the shop. The morning light was making its way in through the skylights and flooding the room.

Tab looked around the room. "It's too bad I'm working for you today. The light's really good."

Benjamin smiled. He was thrilled Tab had learned how important good light was to his project.

Even an overcast day made a big difference in the light level in the shop.

"If you want to trade me a day, you can finish your drawer, but tomorrow we're spending the day together with Old Tabner."

"Okay, let's get started."

Benjamin had been working on another side project—a set of six Windsor back chairs that a customer wanted him to make. He was asked to make them look old and distressed to go with an antique table the couple had. They left a table leaf at the shop so he could match the red and black painting on the table.

Shaping the thin spindles and carving out the seat he could do with his eyes closed, but he wanted to wait for the days Tab wasn't working on his highboy to turn the legs and stretchers on the lathe. That would have to wait for now.

While he set up his tools for the highboy, Tab got together the boards that he would use for drawer number six.

Benjamin noted with approval that Tab planed down the bottom and sides to their final thickness and cut them to length. He had yet to make the dovetails that held the drawers together. He would start by marking out the angles before cutting.

The two were focusing on their work when they were interrupted by the ringing of the phone. Tab looked at Benjamin with a smile. "I'm back in the 1850s today, remember? We don't have phones yet!"

Benjamin smiled back as he turned to grab the phone. "Hello, Kirkman's," he said in a loud voice. "Yes, Mr. Mendenhall, what can I do for you?"

"I'm calling about my dry sink."

Benjamin reached for his clipboard. "It looks like we're going to get started on that in a few weeks."

"I was wondering if we could put a flat TV in it. My wife doesn't have anything from this century in her two-hundred-year-old living room, you see."

"You want it to do what? Come up from the back … I'll have Tab look into that. He loves those kinds of challenges."

"Will this change the cost?"

"Some. We'll adjust the billing for the extra work."

"All right."

"Okay, we'll talk to you soon. Have a great day … good-bye."

Tab stopped working and had a puzzled look on his face. "What was that all about?"

Benjamin relayed the conversation to him. "And since you know a lot more about flat TVs than I do, I think this is a perfect project for you to take the lead."

"Okay … Sounds like a cool project. I can do a little research on the gizmo that the … and they're called flat-screen TVs … go up and down on. Yeah, I think it will be a fun project."

"All right, it's all yours. I'm looking forward to seeing what you come up with."

Tab turned back to his drawings. He had to work on the layout of the dovetail joints for the drawers. The Kirkmans had used the same layout as part of their signature ever since old Tabner's time. Three evenly spaced and the bottom two about one inch apart—the same layout as all the Kirkman drawers.

Tab once had asked Benjamin why they made the two dovetails close together at the bottom.

His answer was, "Maybe Floyd thought it made the drawer stronger, where the bottom was set into a groove in the sides, or he just liked the way it looked."

Tab said, "I like the idea that it was a family tradition."

Benjamin had never been prouder.

An hour later, work was in full swing when Isabella appeared in the Kirkman workshop. She entered so quietly that neither of them noticed she was there until she said, "I have more coffee. Would you like some?"

Both of them stopped working, looking a little startled by her sudden appearance out of nowhere, but they were very happy to see her.

Tab hopped off his stool and brought his empty mug over, "Thank you. I thought you'd sleep until noon at least."

"No, I'm wide awake. I think it'll take a few days to get over the jetlag."

"Well, come on in and make yourself at home." Benjamin offered her a seat. "Would you like to stay awhile?"

"Sure," she said with a look of contentment. "Right now, there's no other place I'd rather be."

She sat at Benjamin's desk and looked around the shop; it felt so good to be in such a familiar place. The brightly lit space and the smell of freshly cut wood took her back to that day many years ago when she first spent the afternoon in the shop with Benjamin.

She remembered how effortlessly he cut the claw-foot chair legs, but she could see that time had not been kind to her old friend. He stopped several times to rub some strength back into his hands. It made her sad to think that someone who could make such lovely things would have such a struggle.

She moved over to Tab's side of the shop and watched him trim the templates he was making for the dovetail layout. She could see he wasn't going to be satisfied until it was perfect. Isabella was happy for Tab; he seemed so confident in his work. The two dressers behind her were taking up a big part of the shop, and she could see one was old and the other was just being built.

"What's going on with these two big dressers?"

Tab launched into the explanation about his challenge and the journey of the old Tabner piece.

As Tab rattled on, she wondered what it would have been like if she had stayed. Would she and Tab be together? Would she have fixed things with her mom and Celeste? It took all her strength to push away her self-doubt and focus on what Tab was saying when he said, "Isabella, do you have anything planned for today?"

His question nudged her out of her funk. "I spent the last three years working to pay off my student loans. As of today, I am debt free, but I need to find a job and a place to live as soon as I can."

Benjamin said, "You're welcome to use Ellen's room as long as you want. In fact, take your time. I'm looking forward to more of your Italian cooking and maybe even some Chinese cooking too."

She laughed. "I'd love to cook that for you. Today I thought I would get started with my job search and open a new bank account. I'll go get my laptop so I can spend the morning here in the shop surfing the internet."

Tab grinned and said, "The internet won't arrive at the shop for another hundred years or so. You'll have to go to the library or one of the coffee shops."

Isabella started to laugh.

Tab smiled wide again and said, "At least we don't have to make our coffee on the old potbellied stove."

Isabella started to laugh again. "You know, Tab, you look just like your grandfather when you smile … I love it."

"Okay, okay, enough of that. The library is that way." He pointed out the window, trying to suppress another smile.

Benjamin said, "You're welcome to use my car."

"No, I can't. I never got a driver's license."

"Oh, I'm sorry. Of course you haven't. I'll be happy to take you wherever you want to go," Benjamin offered.

"Thanks, but I think I'll go for a walk downtown." She topped off both of their coffee mugs and headed back to Ellen's room to get ready.

Isabella had been on a mission for the last seven years. Her trip home from Macau was the completion of that mission. She was a little unsure about what was to come next.

She wondered whether she really felt up to any kind of adventure today. It was almost midnight back in Macau, and she was always in bed by then. How strange it felt to feel so groggy in the middle of the day.

She sat in the chair at the end of the bed and held her coffee mug on her knee, wondering about her family. Isabella noticed there were several new pictures hanging on the far wall. She smiled as she saw her niece and nephew with her sister and Willy. She was a little sad that she had never visited. The rift between Isabella and her sister kept them from talking.

Tab had told her about the babies—a niece and nephew she'd never met—and how Celeste and Willy had become great parents. She regretted not making an effort to get past their differences and knew that had to change.

She didn't want to spend the rest of her life feeling angry at her sister and mother. She had made a decision while she was away to try to forgive and make an attempt at reuniting with her family. It all felt new to her.

Isabella laughed when she saw a photo of herself at the Great Wall of China with that old key hanging around her neck.

There were several photos with Tab and Willy holding the kids and one with Benjamin and Tab. The family resemblance was striking, both with their wide grins and blond hair swept across their foreheads. She let herself daydream about what it would be like if she and Tab had become a couple—something she tried not to think about when she was in Macau. She continually convinced herself Tab was far from being ready for a relationship.

It felt great to verbally spar with Tab. It was a bit like old times, but maybe a little bit too much. Tab had grown into a strong, attractive man, but she knew he still carried that deep emotional wound from the loss of his parents. She could sense in his letters that time had not healed that wound, and maybe it never would.

Isabella could see they both needed to work on their past, overcome burdens, and try to make the best of their lives.

She shook off her grogginess, determined to push through it and accomplish something. She took another sip of coffee, grabbed her things, and headed upstairs to shower.

It was time to start making a new life.

Tab could see the day was coming to an end as the setting sun painted the shop with long shadows. He knew it was time to grab the broom and sweep the shop when the shadows covered his bench.

The days to work on the highboy were growing shorter and shorter. The *Farmer's Almanac* said the days would lose almost two hours of light during October.

He was starting to feel the urgency that old Tabner must have felt as the countryside changed from green to its showy red and gold.

His grandfather's bench was surrounded by mounds of white pine shavings that he had made while planing the replacement bottom and sides of the drawer for old Tabner's highboy.

Tab grabbed the large aluminum dust pan and scooped up the shavings, adding them to the waist bin marked *Compost*.

His grandfather hated to throw anything away that he could use, especially the shavings. They could be added to the garden in the spring.

The last slivers of useful light were almost gone as Tab finished with the broom. He wondered what Isabella was doing. He hadn't seen her return from town.

"Another day in the books," his grandfather remarked as they headed out the door.

As they entered the house, the aroma of garlic and basil filled the room. Tab was surprised to see Isabella was hard at work in the kitchen, stirring a pot of tomato sauce with a wooden spoon.

His grandfather rubbed his hands together and said, "Tab, we're in for a real treat!"

Isabella turned from the stove. "I was wondering when you were coming in. Wash your hands and set the table. Dinner is almost ready."

They did as they were told. Tab even got out his grandmother's candlesticks. Soon there was nothing left to do but sit at the table and wait. Isabella seemed to have it under control, piling generous helpings of spaghetti on each plate topped with her family's favorite meat sauce.

Tab watched her confident movements, feeling surprised and a little dazed.

"The table setting looks nice." Isabella set each plate on the table and took her seat.

His grandfather reached over and put his hand on Tab's arm and said, "I would like to say a blessing if it's okay with you."

Tab nodded once as Isabella said, "Oh, please. I wish you would."

They joined hands and completed the circle around the table. His grandfather smiled and bowed his head.

"Lord, we thank you for this beautiful day and for the work you provide for us. We thank you for Isabella's safe return. Lord, guide her as she prepares for her future. Lord, bless this food to our use and thus to thy service. In Jesus's name we pray, amen."

Isabella whispered a quiet, "Amen," and, "Thank you," as she squeezed their hands. Tab looked quietly over at her. He was a little surprised by her action.

"Okay, dig in before it gets cold."

Tab took his first bite and sat back in his chair. "Oh, man, did I miss this!"

Isabella smiled.

His grandfather said, "I thought you would be running out of steam by now with the jetlag."

"Oh, I did long ago. I was at the coffee shop returning some emails, and by two o'clock I was ready for a nap, so I made my way back and crawled under the covers for a few minutes. When I woke up, I thought I would make some dinner. I need to earn my keep anyway."

"Besides," she added, "I'm thrilled to have someone to cook for.

My roommate spent most nights with her boyfriend, so I spent most evenings alone."

Tab had always thought she was busy, especially when her letters became infrequent. He didn't realize that maybe she had been just as lonely as he was.

Seeming to sense his thoughts, Isabella shrugged. "I had different goals. Staying home with a book was more important than a crazy nightlife."

Tab enjoyed the evening. This was the most life his grandfather's house had seen since they were in high school.

After they finished dinner, Isabella had to give in to her jetlag and head off to bed. Before she did, she approached Tab at the sink while he washed the dishes. "Are you busy tomorrow afternoon? I thought we could spend some time together."

He gave her a small smile. "Sounds like a plan."

A little later, Tab headed back to his apartment, feeling lighter than he had in ages. He was looking forward to spending the day with Isabella. It would be the first time the two of them would be alone in more than six years.

He hoped they could continue where they left off all those years ago, but six years was a long time, and he'd had so little contact with her. He just didn't know what to expect.

Daylight came right on time just like the *Farmer's Almanac* said it would. Tab headed to his bench to wait for the flood of light to pour into the workshop.

His grandfather was already in the shop as expected, with his third cup of coffee, ready to start laying out the dovetails on the restoration.

"Another good day with the light, don't you think?" Tab said. "Maybe it's appropriate we do this repair on old Tabner's highboy with the lights off in honor of the old man."

"Tab, I think that's a fine idea. If you have your plane sharpened, you can take those pine drawer sides and trim them down to size."

"I'm on it."

Isabella brought over a fresh pot of coffee about nine o'clock, which was a welcome interruption.

She sat and watched Tab measure and make marks on the boards that would become the sides of the drawer.

After a while, she asked, "Why do you have to make dovetails? Why can't you just glue and nail it together?"

"It would never last … It would fall apart."

"Why do the dovetails hold it together better than nails?"

"Somehow, someone figured out a long time ago that if you build a drawer with dovetails, it is very hard to pull apart," Tab explained. "In fact, as you pull on the handles of the drawer front, it actually makes the dovetails squeeze tighter together. Nails and glue alone over time pull apart."

He got up from his bench and led her to the old Tabner highboy. He opened one of the drawers. "See, this drawer is more than 150 years old, and it is as solid as the day it was made."

Isabella looked at him with new eyes, seeming impressed with his knowledge.

Noon couldn't have come too soon for Tab. It was time for the two of them to head off for an afternoon together. Tab had been waiting a long time for this day.

They climbed into Tab's car.

"We have a lot to do," said Isabella.

Tab headed out of the driveway. "What do you want to do first?"

"I need to get a phone."

Isabella spent almost two hours selecting a phone and trying to figure out the best plan. This wasn't what he had in mind when she said she wanted to spend the afternoon together, but he did his best to make suggestions when she asked and reassured her she could take all the time she needed when she apologized for taking so long.

Even though he hoped they could start where they left off, he knew she was different.

"All right, I have a phone! What's your number? You're the first person I'm going to call!"

She held out her phone and fumbled to pull up the right screen to add his number. Tab stood close and pointed, "Just slide your finger across the screen … Okay, do it again … There you go. Now just fill in the blanks."

Isabella started typing in *Tab* and then finished with *ner.* "I think I'm going to think of you as Tabner from now on. Okay, what's your number?"

As Tab recited his number to Isabella, he became self-conscious of how close he was standing to her. He stepped back, a little surprised she hadn't created space between them herself. She would have never allowed that before she left.

Isabella looked up at him and started to smile. "What?" she said as she felt his stare.

"Nothing … What's next?"

"Parallel parking!"

"What?"

"I want you to teach me how to parallel park."

Tab tried to hide his unwillingness to let anyone else drive his beloved Mustang, especially to learn how to parallel park, but this was Isabella. Tab had to keep his cool and not let on he was scared to death to let her take the wheel.

"Okay … Let me think," he began. "I know the guy who ran the driving school leaves his cones out all the time so his students can practice with their parents. If no one is there, I'm sure he wouldn't mind if we used them."

She skipped to his car with excitement.

Tab knew she had gone to driving school when she was in high school, but she never got the chance to get her license. She knew the basics, but she struggled to parallel park.

After they arrived at the driving school, Tab stood off to the side ready to give suggestions when she needed them. To his surprise, after a few tries, she had it down.

Tab walked over to the driver's side window and said, "If you can do that one more time, I think you've got it."

"No problem!"

She pulled the car around again and into reverse, lined up the cones, and pulled into the space like a pro.

Tab grinned and nodded his head with approval. "Not bad … Not bad at all."

She opened the door and held out the keys with two fingers and dropped them in Tab's palm. "I never had a doubt."

Tab's smile disguised his relief. His car was still in one piece.

Isabella said, "I downloaded the state driver's booklet when I was still in China. I memorized it so the written test would be a piece of cake."

"Okay, what's next?"

"I think it's time we go somewhere and talk," she said in a serious tone.

Tab wasn't sure what to make of her comment, but he could see her mood had quickly turned. He had been waiting for this moment ever since Isabella sent her last letter. He suggested they go to the coffee shop that was at the bookstore. They could sit and talk for as long as they wanted, but she wanted pizza—specifically, New York-style pizza.

"That's another thing you can't get in China. They just can't get the cheese right."

Tab knew right where to go—an old hole-in-the-wall pizza joint they used to go to when they were in high school.

"Classic pepperoni with double cheese like old times?" asked Tab.

"You know it!"

They sat down at one of the smaller tables. Tab placed their order and got a couple of Cokes.

Tab had much to say but didn't know where to start. "I'm glad you wanted to come home and this is where you came home to. You seem ... surer of yourself."

She smiled. "I feel that way. I spent all those years in school and in China angry with my sister and my mother. I thought it was their weaknesses that made me want to never be like them, but instead, I discovered my own weaknesses."

"What do you mean?"

"I started thinking about my sister and her kids and how I was missing out on watching them grow up. And where is my mother now, and is she okay? I realized I still cared. I had to come home and try to make things right with Celeste and my mom. I need my family back."

Tab sat there for a while trying to take in what Isabella had said. He was happy for her, of course, but felt sad too. Deep down, he hoped that he was part of the reason she decided to come home. Then he chided himself.

"I talk to Willy all the time. Maybe I can help somehow. You know,

Celeste is a great mom; she can barely string two sentences together without saying something about her kids."

"Tab, that would be great. Thank you. What about you? How are you doing?"

The arrival of pizza saved him from answering.

Isabella leaned in and inhaled a lungful of the most incredible smelling pizza in West Hartford.

Tab tried to slide a slice onto a paper plate, but it was almost too hot to touch. He handed it to Isabella and then took one for himself. She folded her slice in half and took her first bite of real pizza in three years.

Tab laughed as a long string of cheese hung from her chin.

She smiled with her mouth full and slapped Tab on the forearm.

"Do you know what else is hard to get in China? Grilled cheese sandwiches—my favorite."

"Another cheese and bread item. I'm sensing a theme here."

They laughed and joked their way through the meal. She talked about all the things she had looked forward to when she got back to the States. Tab watched her every move and hung on every word until there was only one slice left. Neither one of them was able to take another bite.

Isabella said, "Let's head back to your grandfather's house and sit on the porch like old times."

The drive home was only ten minutes, but it felt like hours to Tab. Although they were having a good time, Tab still felt like things were unfinished between them.

His grandfather was sitting at the kitchen table working on some of his bookkeeping when they arrived.

As Isabella went to her room to grab a sweater, Tab stopped to tell his grandfather they were going to sit out on the porch for a while.

"Well, that would be wonderful," he said.

Tab tried not to read too much into his grandfather's grin.

Isabella emerged, and he followed her outside. She took her place on the porch swing, and Tab pulled the chair around so they could see each other. She tucked up one of her legs under the other and wrapped her sweater tightly around her as the evening grew chilly.

Again, they sat there, each waiting for the other to start. From the day he received her letter, he couldn't make any sense of her long silence. He had given up on ever seeing her again … and now …

"You know, I wasn't sure I was ever going to see you again. I sent you letter after letter that you never answered. Did I do something wrong?"

She sat there for a few moments, biting on her fingernail. "No, Tab. You did everything right."

"Then what was it?"

She looked out at the night. "I was so homesick that I had to isolate myself from anything that made me want to pack up and come home. I had to finish what I started, and when I was asked to stay another six months, I knew that I could finish paying off my school loan. It would also give me the money I would need to get started when I came home. I had to stop reading your letters. I couldn't think about anything but work. It worked for a while, but I started thinking about you." She turned back to him with tears streaming down her cheeks. "Are you still the Tab I remember?"

"I'm still the same Tab."

"Oh." Her voice quieted, as if he hadn't given her the right answer. "How are you really?"

"Oh, I'm good. I'm just fine, even better now that you're back."

It didn't take much effort for Isabella to see through his bravado, but he was relieved when she let it go.

She shivered in her sweater and pulled it even more tightly around her.

"You're freezing," he said. "Maybe we should—"

"I'm okay."

"You look tired too. Come on. We'll have plenty of time to catch up. Let's go inside."

She nodded reluctantly.

Isabella did her best to dry her tears, passing him as he held the door for her.

Tab had a thousand thoughts running through his head. He had no idea what he should do or say. He just wanted to spend time with his old friend, just like he used to.

They entered the kitchen to say good night to his grandfather, who was still doing paperwork at the table.

His grandfather invited Tab to church as he always did. Tab respectfully declined as always.

Isabella chimed in. "I would like to come if I can."

Tab looked at her with surprise and irritation.

His grandfather grinned. "Well, I'm happy to have someone come along with me after going all these years by myself."

Tab screwed a smile on his face. "Okay, good night you two. Isabella, I'll see you tomorrow." He slipped out the door unnoticed.

Tab grumbled to himself all the way home.

Isabella sat with Benjamin in his usual spot in the back row of the church. He explained how it was the closest seat to his car and how every step he didn't have to take was a blessing these days.

Benjamin offered to make her lunch after church. "I can't tell you how long it's been since I've had someone to have lunch with after church."

Isabella enjoyed her time with Benjamin that Sunday. She told him how she wanted to talk to her sister and how she wanted to find out where her mother was.

Benjamin said, "I think you will be surprised. Celeste and Willy are different people. They aren't high school kids any more. They are responsible adults and wonderful parents. I think they would love to hear from you."

"I don't know. I was so awful to her."

"What do you have to lose?"

Isabella conceded that he had a point. "What about my mom? Do you think Celeste might know where she is?"

Benjamin said, "I don't know if Celeste knows where she is, but I do."

"You do? Where is she?"

"She's here in West Hartford. She's changed a lot too. I know she isn't drinking anymore and that she's remarried."

"How do you know?"

"She goes to my church."

Isabella felt a jolt of surprise. "I can't believe it! Are you sure?"

"Sure, I'm sure. She was there today. She was sitting in the front row where she always sits with her new husband." He paused. "I wasn't sure if you wanted to know. I'm sorry."

Isabella waved off the apology. She had a hundred things running through her mind; most of them were memories of her mother. The most disturbing thought was that they were in the same place, and her mother hadn't even see her.

She sat looking out the kitchen window, not knowing what to say with tears rolling down her cheeks.

Benjamin reached across the table and took her hand. "It's okay. I know it's going to work out. When you have the chance to change something, take it."

Benjamin was right. Isabella called her sister that afternoon, and to her surprise, Celeste was overjoyed by her call. Celeste invited her to Germany to stay as long as she could. Soon they would be coming home for a week to spend with Willy's parents during Thanksgiving.

Benjamin found her that afternoon on the porch swing.

"Hey, young lady, why the tears? You sounded so happy on the phone. I would have thought you would have run out of tears by now."

She looked up at him with a big smile and patted the seat next to her. "Please, come sit with me." She wiped her tears with the sleeve of her sweater. Don't let these tears fool you. I'm so happy I called. It's like I've been missing a part of me. I guess that twin thing, where you feel each other, is true even if you're on the other side of the world. I think I even shared her cravings and labor pains when she had the babies."

They both laughed, but Isabella started to tear up again. "I got to talk to my niece and nephew. Little Chloe even called me mommy and started to cry. It must have been a little confusing looking at her mom and then hearing her voice over the phone. I could hear Celeste assuring her that it was okay. She was hearing her Aunt Isabella, mommy's sister. After a while, she thought it was so funny. You should have heard her giggle … She was so cute!"

"I'm so glad your call went so well."

Isabella wiped another tear from her cheek. "I feel so bad! I've missed watching them grow up. All that time was lost."

Benjamin strongly disagreed. "No, dear! It wasn't wasted, not a bit of it. You've learned a lot about yourself and what's important to you. There's something special about family. They can hurt you more than anyone else, but they also have the capacity to forgive and forget quickly."

He patted her on the knee and said, "I think you're going to have a great time making up for the time you've been away." Benjamin's knees creaked as he stood. "Just think of all the fun you'll have spoiling them."

Over the next few days, Isabella and Celeste had several conversations, catching up on the last few years.

Willy made arrangements for Isabella to sublet his aunt's house while she spent the winter in Florida. Isabella knew she couldn't stay in Ellen's room forever and was delighted with the offer.

The one thing they couldn't agree on was their mother.

Celeste wasn't ready to let go of her anger. Their mother had called and written Celeste several times over the years, but she refused to talk to her or even read her letters.

Isabella told her about Benjamin's advice, but she still wasn't interested.

Isabella decided to go ahead and contact her mother and hope for the best. With Benjamin's help, she got her phone number and made the decision to call her after dinner that night.

She put on her coat and went out to sit on the porch swing. She took a deep breath and dialed the number before she lost her nerve.

After a few rings, a male voice answered. "Hello?"

Isabella's mind went blank for a second.

"Hello?"

She swallowed again and with a dry mouth said, "Yes, this is Isabella Sabatini. I would like to talk to my mother, please."

"Praise God! We have been praying for this day for a long time. Please wait one minute. I'll get her. She's in the basement doing laundry."

Isabella could hear the thumps of footsteps as he went to get her mother.

Then she heard her mother's quivering voice. "Isabella … Isabella, honey … Is it really you?"

She could feel her heart ache and melt as she heard her mother's voice say her name. With a tearful voice, she said, "Yes, Mommy, it's me."

Isabella struggled to say more.

Her mother saved her the trouble. "It's okay … It's okay … I'm so happy you called. I've missed you so much."

Isabella took a big breath and tried to compose herself so she could talk. "I've missed you too, Mom. I want to see you. I want us to be a family again if we can. I'm tired of being so lonely."

"I'm here now. I'm sorry I wasn't there when you needed me. I'm so … sorry."

The ache in Isabella's heart lifted. They made arrangements to meet the next day for coffee at the diner. They said tearful good nights.

Isabella was so nervous about meeting her mom the following afternoon that she could hardly stand it. She hung out in the shop with Tab and Benjamin for a while trying to keep her mind occupied with something else.

Soon it was time to go.

Tab offered to drive her, but Isabella wanted to walk.

When she entered the diner, she saw her mother sitting in the corner booth with her back to the door. Isabella walked over and put her hand on her mother's shoulder.

Her mom sprung to her feet and wrapped her arms around her. They stood there in a never-ending embrace, neither wanting to let go. Then she stood back to get a good look at Isabella. "You're so beautiful! Look at you … so very beautiful," she said as her voice tapered off.

Isabella could see the years had been hard on her. She smiled as her mom put her hands on both sides of her face and said, "It's so good to see you. Let's sit and talk."

Isabella told her mom about college and living in China and how the long separation from her family made her want to come home and find a way to reconcile her relationships with the family.

"So, tell me about Steve," Isabella said.

"He's such a wonderful man. I've never felt loved like this before. It makes me feel so blessed to have someone so special in my life. He can't wait to meet you."

Then her mom got serious. "I want to tell you how sorry I am for all the pain I caused you and your sister. I know I wasn't the mom you needed. As a recovering alcoholic, I learned at my AA meetings that I had to make a list of all the people I hurt with my addiction and how I needed to make amends.

"You and Celeste are the last on my list and the two I needed to make the biggest apologies to."

"Mom, you went to AA?"

"You bet! I had to; it was a condition of my sentencing for drunk driving."

Isabella put her hand over her mouth with shock and concern. "Drunk driving?" She hoped her mother hadn't caused an accident—or worse. She thought of Tab's parents.

"Don't worry. The only person I hurt was myself. I was a mess. After the two of you left, I really went off the deep end. I got two DUIs in three weeks, and I was even willing to blame it all on you and Celeste ... Pretty crazy, huh?"

"Mom, that's awful."

"You bet it was. I had a long road ahead of me. I was bitter, defiant, and mad, but mostly mad. After a lot of work and a few setbacks, I've been sober now for three years."

Isabella listened intently to her mom as she described her journey through AA's twelve-step program. It was hard to believe she could've been any worse than when she was still living at home. She could feel her mother had changed, and now she felt badly she hadn't been around to help her when she needed it.

Her mom stopped and took a drink of her now-cold coffee. "Enough about me. Now that you're here, what plans do you have?"

"I'm still settling in, but I hope to find a teaching position in the local schools, possibly teaching English as a second language."

"What about Tab Kirkman? Are you still spending time with him?"

Isabella sunk down in the booth. "Our friendship and special arrangement were the things that kept me grounded for so long."

"What special arrangement?"

She told her mom about the pact that she made with him all those years ago, being a platonic couple, and how he vowed to never get close to anyone ever again.

"By the time I got to China, he was all I could think about. It took all my strength to stay and finish my mission. When I got back, he made it clear he was still the same Tab, with the same bitter feelings he had at sixteen. I'm not sure he's ever going to be ready to let it go and have a real relationship."

"He's the best friend you've ever had," said her mother.

"He is my best friend … and I don't know if I'm in love with him or I'm in love with the thought of him. Anyway, we'll never get the chance to figure it all out if he's not even willing to take the step from friend to dating … and worst of all, I'm scared if I push him at all, I'll … You know … I just can't bear to lose what I've got."

Isabella took a deep breath and half smiled and half sighed. Her mom reached across the table to her in a reassuring gesture.

They talked for hours and looked forward to seeing each other again.

Isabella promised to bring photos of Celeste's kids the next time they got together, determined to help her make contact with Celeste.

As they left the diner, they hugged each other, finding it difficult to let go. Isabella waved to her mother as she drove off. She was so happy for her. She felt a completeness she hadn't felt for nearly half her life.

Tab was still at the house when Isabella returned, anxious to hear the details of her meeting with her mother.

He had been sitting on the porch for hours. He ducked into the house quickly when he saw her coming and returned with a soda for each of them.

As Isabella stepped onto the porch, he could see how happy she was. "Well, how'd it go?"

She sat on the porch swing with Tab and gave it a big push. With her hands clasped together, she closed her eyes for a moment and then turned to Tab. "This is the best day of my life. I never in a million years would have thought I would ever see my mom sober or dressed like an adult. I fully expected to see her in a bar or something, but she's alive … and well … and happy, really happy!"

Tab smiled back at her and said, "I'm really, really happy for you. I know you've had mixed feelings about seeing her again."

He did his best to keep his smile and enthusiasm for everything she experienced during their afternoon together. He even asked her the same question twice.

"So, you're probably going to spend a lot of time with her, don't you think?"

"Oh, I guess so … I haven't thought about it that much … I would like to try helping my mom and Celeste work things out."

Tab's old feelings started to invade his thoughts.

Isabella had her sister back and her mom, and she was happy. He wondered how he was going to fit in with her new life too. In Tab's eyes, all Isabella's problems were gone. She had no reason to stick to their pact. He started to feel like he was losing her, even though she didn't say anything of the kind. His imagination was in full swing. All he wanted was for the two of them to go back to the way it was, nothing more, nothing less.

Not wanting the misery to show on his face, Tab made an excuse of needing to do laundry so he could escape before he felt worse than he already did.

"I'll see you in the morning Isabella," Tab mumbled under his breath.

The October weather was going to be gray and rainy for the next few days, even though the *Farmer's Almanac* said otherwise. It was just as well. Tab was looking forward to taking a few days off from working on his highboy to help his grandfather on another set of six Windsor back chairs.

The week was uneventful for Tab and his grandfather in the shop, but not for Isabella. She had purchased a car that her new stepfather found for her, and she passed her driver's test. She had moved into Willy's aunt's house over the weekend, which made her transition complete. All she needed now was a job.

Tab had expected Isabella wouldn't be around now that she had a place to stay, but to his surprise, she still came over every day and hung out in the shop.

She also had dinner with them on most evenings.

Tab was willing to take whatever time Isabella was willing to give, and he hoped it was enough.

Chapter 11

❧

The Fall

THE RESTORATION OF OLD TABNER'S highboy was nearly finished. Tab had planed the white pine drawer sides down to thickness by hand to keep the look of the repair the same as the rest of the old dresser.

Benjamin repaired the small chips in the face and cut the dovetails in the new drawer sides. His final task was to adjust the drawer so it would fit flush to the cabinet.

Even though he was more than six feet tall, Benjamin still needed to stand on a stool to get the best view of his work. Every time he stepped off the stool, he felt a shooting pain in his neglected knees. He bit his lip to hide the wince.

Tab noticed his wince and asked, "Are you sure you don't want me to do that? It looks like your knees are really painful today."

Benjamin, making light of it, said, "I know the doctor insisted I consider getting new knees, but I would really like to keep my own."

Another day had come and gone, and Tab and Isabella again made plans to spend the evening out.

"Are you sure you don't want to join us, Benjamin?" Isabella asked.

"Oh, no. I'm going to spend just a few more minutes here and then enjoy a quiet evening catching up on some reading."

"All right, but take it easy," said Tab.

Isabella kissed him on the cheek.

He sat on his stool and watched as they headed off for their evening together. He still hoped the two of them would get together, but it seemed uncertain. Things had fallen into place pretty quickly for Isabella since she arrived home. She had even gotten a job like she hoped, teaching English as a second language. On the other hand, Benjamin had real concerns about Tab.

Benjamin looked at the clock and stood to do the final fit of the repaired drawer, but a sharp pain forced him back to his seat. He shook his head as he rubbed his aching knees.

He was feeling a little regretful for not taking his doctor's advice. Knee replacements were inevitable, but it never felt right leaving Tab in the shop alone. It would be a minimum of six weeks before he could get back in the shop to work.

Now that Tab was nearly finished with his project, it may be the right time. Tab would continue running the business without his constant presence.

Benjamin pressed himself up again from his stool and stood in front of the two highboys. He felt pride for what his young apprentice had accomplished and whispered a soft, "Beautiful."

A feeling of melancholy washed over him as he thought about his Ellen, Charles, and Elizabeth and how proud they would be too.

He looked over the fine detail and flawless workmanship. "Tab, my boy ... This is really something. I think my time here is almost complete." There was no doubt in his mind Tab was ready to take his place as master craftsman.

He was determined to finish fitting the drawer—just a few more shavings, and the fit should be perfect. He stepped up on the stool and slid the drawer into place, checking the fit.

"Almost got it ... just a little bit more." But when he stepped off the stool once more, a burst of pain overwhelmed him.

Tab was heading home late after his night out with Isabella. The Dollar Theater had a Vincent Price film festival the night before Halloween, and the finale of the festival was *House of Wax*. They had both watched it on television but thought it would be fun to see it at the theater.

He was happy to have the time alone with her. Tab convinced himself that it was only a matter of time before she drifted away from him. Now that she had her family back, she wouldn't need him anymore. He felt conflicted between his need to be with Isabella and his teenage vow to never get close to anybody. He made every effort to enjoy every minute with her, not knowing when it would end.

It was almost one thirty in the morning by the time he dropped her off at Willy's aunt's house. On his way home, he passed by his grandfather's shop.

He was surprised to still see a light on.

Tired after a long night, he didn't think anything of it at first, but by the time he pulled on to his street, the feeling that something wasn't right made it impossible for him to get a moment of sleep. His grandfather shouldn't be working so late, and if he wasn't working? Tab knew how his grandfather hated to waste anything, including electricity.

He went back to make sure everything was all right.

As he pulled up to the shop, he could see through the shop window that the little desk lamp on his grandfather's bench was still on.

He quietly entered the house to get the skeleton key, making sure he didn't wake him up, but the key wasn't in its usual place. He walked back to the shop door and put his hand up to the window, straining to look into the mostly dark room. Not seeing anything out of place, he decided to head home. Before he left, he checked the door to make sure it was locked. To his surprise, it was unlocked. He instantly felt uneasy. He could see his grandfather forgetting a light, but not locking the door, never.

He cautiously stepped into the shop and heard a low moan. After a night of Vincent Price movies, the sound was pretty eerie.

Tab didn't know what to make of the sound at first as he continued to look around. There was no one behind him.

Then he peered down and saw his grandfather lying on the floor halfway under one of the benches.

"Grandpa!" He dropped to his knees to be at his grandfather's side. "Grandpa, what happened?"

His grandfather moaned again.

Tab put his hand on his grandfather's shoulder and started to role him over.

"No, don't touch me ... I broke something ... my leg ... oh, my leg." His grandfather moaned even louder.

Tab looked down at Benjamin's right leg and was mortified to see his foot turned at an unnatural angle. Tab scooted around so he could see his grandfather's face and saw a huge gash in his forehead.

Fear and confusion welled up in Tab. He grabbed his phone from his pocket and fumbled to dial 9-1-1.

Tab rattled off the address, and the dispatcher said, "We have an ambulance en route to your location."

Tab fought to keep his composure. "What can I do?" he asked the dispatcher in a panicked voice.

"Stay with him, and it's important that you do not move him. I'll stay on the line until the ambulance arrives."

After just a few minutes, Tab could hear sirens. "I hear the siren!" he said to the dispatcher.

He jumped to his feet and ran outside and waved at the rescue squad as they pulled into the drive.

The dispatcher said, "I will let you work with them now."

Tab propped open the door of the workshop as a man and woman jumped out of the squad, grabbed their gear, and ran into the shop.

Upon seeing them, his grandfather said slowly in a weak voice, "My leg ..." as he started to move his hand to his hip.

"Okay, sir. I want you to lie still for me."

The other EMT reached into one of his boxes for a cervical collar, handed it to his partner, and then moved around to the other side to help hold Benjamin's neck still as he secured the collar. They worked quickly to get his vital signs and asked him questions to assess his condition.

One of the EMTs looked at Tab. "Are you injured too?"

"No! I just found him and called," he said, confused by the question.

Just as they finished, two more men from the fire department walked in ready to help. The woman looked up at Tab and said, "Can we move this table that he's under? It would help us get him out of here."

"Oh ... sure," said Tab, relieved to tear his eyes from the scene and do something to help. He removed the chair parts that were stacked on top of it. "We can take him straight out the door."

The two firefighters each took an end of the table and lifted it up and over the other benches straight out the shop door. The EMTs worked quickly as they prepared Benjamin for transport to the hospital.

Tab's grandfather cried in pain as they rolled him on his side and lifted him onto the gurney. Tab's eyes watered at the horrible sound, and he clenched his teeth as the stress of the moment overwhelmed him. Once they got Benjamin in the rescue squad, they gave him oxygen and started an IV. They rushed toward the emergency room with their flashing lights illuminating the neighborhood and siren blaring.

Tab jumped in his car and followed them as the comments made by the EMTs replayed in his head, things like low blood pressure, possible concussion, and blood loss from a possible broken hip.

He tried not to think about what all those things might add up to and how this day was going to end. The feelings of being alone again, like he had all those years ago, were starting to creep into his mind.

The ambulance disappeared in the distance, while he was stopped by traffic lights one after another. Not a single car crossed in front of him as he waited for the lights to change.

By the time he was stopped by the third light, the fear of the unknown was getting the best of him. He pounded the steering wheel of his beloved Mustang in frustration. When he looked and saw that no one was coming, he slammed his foot on the gas pedal. With tires squealing, he fishtailed his way through the intersection.

He didn't let his foot off the gas until he turned into the parking lot of the hospital. He yanked the car one way and then the other and parked it at an angle hanging partly out of the parking spot.

Tab ran from the parking lot into the emergency room entrance, desperate to keep up with his grandfather. Much to his irritation, he had to give the front desk his grandfather's information before he could go back and see what was going on.

By the time he got to his grandfather's side, there were several nurses working to get him stabilized. They had cut his clothes off, which revealed a large dark bruise around his right hip.

Tab wanted to get closer to him, but there were so many people around him that he knew he had to stay out of the way.

A few moments had passed when a doctor came in to assess Benjamin's injuries.

Tab watched as the doctor listened to his heart and then looked at his hip.

The doctor started to ask his grandfather questions. "What is your name? Do you know where you are? Can you tell me what happened?"

His grandfather's answers came slowly. It was clear he was weak and confused.

The doctor looked over at Tab and asked, "Can you tell me what happened?"

Tab said, "I wasn't there when it happened. I think he fell from a step stool and hit his head."

The doctor's attention was on his grandfather as he asked if he knew any medical history. "Does he take any medication?"

"He takes something for high blood pressure and a baby aspirin … and I think he takes something when his knees are hurting him."

"Is it a prescription?"

"I don't think so … No, it's over the counter."

"Do you know who his doctor is?"

"I think it's Dr. Long."

"Dr. Kevin Long?"

"Yes."

The doctor said to one of the nurses, "Get his records." He continued his examination while simultaneously telling the nurse to order an MRI and get someone from orthopedics to come down. The doctor disappeared as quickly as he had appeared.

By then, there were only two nurses in the room, so Tab was able to get closer and take his grandfather's hand. "I'm sorry I wasn't with you earlier. I should have been there for you."

His grandfather just squeezed his hand. "It's not your fault," he said in a faint voice.

Tab's eyes began to tear up again, "I'm so sorry … I shouldn't have left you."

His grandfather slowly shook his head, trying to smile as if Tab was being a knucklehead. "Don't be silly. I'm going to be okay. I want someone here with you. Call the Murphys. They'll come down and stay with you."

"No … Really, I'm okay"

He shook his head again. "Please, Tab. I don't want you to be alone."

"Okay, then I'll call Isabella."

He shook his head again, exhausted from the effort.

Tab stepped away to call. After several rings, it went to voice mail. He quickly redialed the number, anxiously trying to reach Isabella.

"Tab, what is it?" Her voice was soft and groggy.

"It's Grandpa … He fell." Tab could feel his throat tighten, but he took a deep breath and told Isabella what happened. "He's in the emergency room, and he's got to have emergency surgery."

Isabella said in a troubled voice, "Oh no! I'm on my way right now!" and ended the call without another word.

He turned back to his grandfather and took his hand. "Isabella's coming. She should be here soon."

His grandfather squeezed his hand and, in a whisper, said, "Good."

After a few minutes, two more men arrived to take him for his MRI.

Tab followed as they twisted and turned their way through the hospital. At the end of the hall, one of the men said to Tab, "This is as far as you go. We'll let you know when we've brought him back to the emergency room.

Tab stood at the double doors for a few moments, wondering if he could find his way back.

It wasn't only worry that occupied Tab's mind. Deep down, he felt frightened. Ever since his parents died, Tab had lost something in himself.

He remembered the day after his parents' accident.

Tab had walked into his grandfather's kitchen still wearing the clothes he wore to bed.

"What am I going to do? Where am I going to live?" he'd asked his grandfather.

"Tab! We'll start the day however you want. I am here for you if you need to talk to someone or have someone here with you … We'll make the call. Tab, we'll get through this!"

"Grandpa, I feel numb. I don't know what to do … I'm lost …"

"Tab, it's okay. It's how you're supposed to feel. We're going to take this one step at a time, hour by hour, day by day."

Little by little, they pieced their lives back together. His grandfather went back to work, and Tab became eager to spend more time in the shop with him. It was the one place where he felt normal, and his grandfather was more than happy to have the help.

As he finished his senior year, he had considered his options, but he felt obligated to stay with his grandfather. He was going through the motions, throwing himself into his work at the shop. While Tab wallowed in his grief to avoid the world, his grandfather helped him to realize the value of his work and of himself.

Tab had grown up a lot since then, and he owed it all to his grandfather.

Tab was still waiting for his grandfather to return from his MRI when he got a text. It was from Isabella. "I'm here, can't come in, not family."

Tab made his way out to the front desk. Isabella's concerned look made his emotions overflow.

"He's okay ... I mean, they're taking care of him."

Tab gave her a blow-by-blow description of what happened. Isabella reached up and touched the side of his face with her fingertips. "Oh my God. Are you hurt too?"

Tab wiped at the spot and felt dried blood. He had no idea he had gotten some of his grandfather's blood on him. Some of the looks that he had gotten since he arrived at the hospital had suddenly started to make sense.

Isabella said, "I want to see him! Get me back there!"

Tab approached the woman behind the desk, still wiping the blood off his face. "Excuse me, ma'am. I need to get a wristband for her so she can be with my grandfather. We're the only family he has."

She quickly made a wristband and placed it on Isabella's wrist. By the time they got back to the room, his grandfather had returned from his MRI.

Isabella and Tab went quickly back to the emergency room where Benjamin was waiting. She kissed him on the forehead and told him, "I love you ... We're here for you."

Nurses were coming and going, taking his pulse, checking his blood pressure, and taking blood. Finally, a nurse came in and took the large bandage off his temple and cleaned it.

She said with a smile, "It's not that bad. I think we only need a couple of Steri-Strips."

Tab said, "I thought he was going to need some stitches."

She looked at it again and said, "Nah … It's not that bad. Head wounds bleed a lot, and they always look worse than they really are."

About twenty minutes later, the orthopedic surgeon came in. After a few minutes of examining his grandfather, he said, "Well, Mr. Kirkman, it looks like we need to take you into surgery as soon as you're ready. Your hip is fractured just below the head. I think we can repair it without a prosthesis, but we're a little concerned about the blood supply to the joint."

He rattled on about how they were going to repair the break and what to expect after surgery. Tab started to hear less and less as the reality of his grandfather's future with him in the shop started to look doubtful. He would, of course, move back into his grandfather's house and into his old bedroom on the second floor.

Was he ready to continue the family business without him? It was more than the work in the shop, much more.

After the surgeon, left, Benjamin, Tab, and Isabella talked about what needed to be done at the shop for the next week.

Isabella said she would be happy to do whatever she could to help out. Benjamin assured the both of them that he was going to be fine and would be back in the shop in no time. Tab and Isabella both agreed with him, knowing the truth to be otherwise but making light of the situation.

As they talked, the hospital staff started to prep him for surgery. The anesthesiologist asked him questions about his medications and allergies and told him what to expect from the procedure. Soon after, Benjamin was taken to surgery.

Tab and Isabella followed as they wheeled him toward the OR. She assured him that she would be waiting for him as she walked beside him trying to keep eye contact. "I'll look after Tab too," she said as she gave him a big, reassuring smile.

The orderly said, "Okay, say your goodbyes," as he pushed the button to open the OR doors.

Tab leaned over and whispered in his ear, "I'll see you soon … I love you." They were words he hadn't said to him in a very long time.

Isabella put her arm around Tab's shoulder. "I'll say a prayer for you, Benjamin." And she blew him a kiss as they watched him disappear behind the OR doors. Isabella squeezed Tab's shoulder. "Let's find the waiting room. Do you want some coffee or something?"

Tab didn't answer. He just followed along, walking as if his feet were made of lead. He found the most secluded corner of the waiting room and sat with his elbows on his knees and his hands over his head.

Isabella sat next to him, motionless. After a few moments, she left her chair.

Tab didn't move. He assumed she went to the vending machine and was relieved to be alone with his overwhelming worry. He broke down and sobbed.

Isabella returned and knelt down in front of Tab, trying to console him as he sobbed uncontrollably.

Not long after Isabella arrived, her mother and stepfather entered the waiting room. Tab looked up at them and then at Isabella.

"I called them," Isabella said to him. "This is Steve."

Tab nodded to them as they took the seats next to him. They assured him they were going to stay with him as long as he needed them.

Isabella's mom whispered loudly to her, "Do you know if Tab called his uncle?"

Isabella shook her head. "I don't know."

Tab sat up and wiped his face with his sleeve. "Aw, crap … crap …" He stood up and took his cell phone from his pocket to dial his uncle.

It went to voice mail. "You have reached the voice mail of Ronny Kirkman. Leave a message after the beep."

He took a big breath and said, "Uncle Ronny, give me a call … Grandpa's in the hospital … He broke his hip … Call me as soon as you can." He dropped the phone to his side and said, "Aw man, I shouldn't have said that!"

Steve stood up and placed his hand on Tab's shoulder. "It's okay, Tab."

Nothing was okay. Tab turned away.

He felt all alone, and that's the way he wanted it to stay. His prediction that everyone he ever loved was going to leave him felt as if it were coming true. Even Isabella had her family back and didn't need him anymore.

"I'm sorry. I need to be alone for a while." He walked to the other side of the room and sat by himself and tried to hide his tears.

He wallowed in self-pity, alone and justified in his solitude. Much to his irritation, an old man dressed in dark clothes with a long white beard and a yarmulke sat in the chair next to him.

Tab did his best to ignore him, but he could see there were many other chairs available around him. *Why did he have to sit right next to me?* he thought. He shifted in his chair to move as far away from him as he could without being openly rude.

Still, the man just sat there.

Tab could hardly stand it. He tried to get a look at him without the man noticing.

Tab could see he had a small string of beads that he continued to turn, one bead at a time. He could hear him whisper so softly that he couldn't make out what he was saying.

Tab's irritation was starting to give way to a strange curiosity about the old man. He watched the beads pass through his fingers one after another.

Both men sat there for nearly an hour, neither speaking to one another.

Curiosity got the best of Tab, and he finally asked about the string of beads. "What is that you have in your hand?"

The man didn't say anything at first. He just continued to turn the beads one after another and whispered quietly. Eventually, he looked over and smiled as he lifted his hand toward Tab. It was a short loop of colored string with several large multicolored beads.

The old man said, "They're just beads. Here, I want you to have them."

"Oh, no thanks. I couldn't."

"I have lots. I *want* you to have them."

Tab held out his hand, and the old man laid them gently in his palm. As Tab looked them over, the old man reached in his pocket and pulled out another string and continued whispering to himself.

Gently fondling the beads to see what it felt like to run them through his fingers like the old man, Tab asked, "What are they for?"

"They're prayer beads. I hold a bead in my fingers and say a prayer to God. Then I turn to the next one and say another prayer."

"I don't pray anymore; they're not going to do me any good." Tab reached out to hand them back.

"I want you to keep them anyway. These beads have already had some answered prayers."

"Oh, yeah? What prayers were answered?" Tab asked with a doubtful tone.

"I prayed you would start a conversation with me, and you did."

"Okay, you got me on that one."

"I know you said you don't pray anymore, but if you did, what would you pray for right now."

Tab thought for a minute. "I would pray that I would wake up and my grandfather would be all right."

The old man didn't speak for a moment. "You know God doesn't work that way, don't you?"

"I thought God could do anything he wants."

"Well, you're right about that. God *can* do anything. Do you think you'll wake up and everything will be all right?"

"No."

They both sat there in the silence of the moment.

Then the old man said, "It looks like your friends over there are praying. What do you think they're praying for?"

"They're praying for my grandfather. He's having emergency surgery to fix his broken hip."

The old man took a longer look at them. "No, that's not it, not it at all," and he got up and without saying another word walked away.

Tab sat there wondering about what he had said. What else would they be praying about if they weren't praying for his grandfather?

He watched the three of them, wondering what they were saying. He could see Isabella was crying as her mom was trying to console her.

Then he noticed he was rolling the beads in his fingers. He looked down at his hand and thought to himself, *If I were to pray, I would want to take away her pain.*

He rolled the beads in his fingers and said, "God, take away her pain." Then he thought that was a crummy prayer, and he thought about his grandfather's prayers. They were like poetry or fine literature. He thought God wouldn't listen to his prayers.

He sat there feeling like it was stupid to have even tried.

He looked over to where Isabella was sitting and saw she was looking right at him. She had stopped crying and didn't take her eyes off of him. He could even see a little smile.

Tab felt a warm rush come over him. She did need his friendship as much as he needed hers. He looked down at the beads in his hand and thought about what he had done.

Tab got up and walked over to her, taking the chair next to her. Neither of them knew what to say, but Tab sensed something unique between them.

An aide approached and told him that his grandfather was in recovery. The doctor would be coming down soon to talk to him and that he should wait in Consultation Room B.

Tab asked them all to come with him.

Soon after they entered the consultation room, the doctor came in and started to describe what was done during surgery.

"We were able to save the hip joint. He had good blood supply to the joint, and I expect he should make a full recovery. We will talk to him about what he will need to help him with his recovery over the next few days. He will be in recovery a little while longer. Check with the information desk, and they will let you know his room number. Do you have any questions?"

Tab asked, "How long it will be before he can walk up the stairs to his bedroom?"

"It'll be several weeks. He may need to stay at a nursing facility to make sure he can get the proper care and rehabilitation."

Isabella and Tab went up to his grandfather's room and waited for him to arrive from recovery. They were both exhausted from their all-night vigil. Tab had no idea what to expect. Before today, he had never even visited a hospital.

Before long, a nurse came in and started to prepare the room. Two other nurses wheeled his grandfather into the room. The sight of his grandfather hooked up to all the tubes and wires startled Tab.

When Tab approached his grandfather, he tried to smile under the oxygen mask as he reached out his hand.

Tab clasped it gently. "Grandpa, how are you feeling?"

"I'm so sleepy. It's hard to stay awake."

Isabella came over and stood next to Tab. She tried to stay out of the way of the nurses as they untangled all the tubes and wires. His grandfather was having a hard time keeping his eyes open. She put her hand on his shoulder and reassured him, saying, "Benjamin, we're both here."

He replied without opening his eyes and weakly waving his hand. "Both of you go home. I'm going to stay right here and get some sleep."

When the nurses had finished, one by one they left the room. The last nurse said to Tab, "You can stay here tonight if you like. The sofa folds out into a bed."

His grandfather refused with the little energy he had left. "No, go home!"

Tab said, "Okay, we'll go home." He bent over and did his best to hug him, despite all the wires in the way.

Isabella leaned in and kissed him on the forehead and whispered in his ear, "Love you," and kissed him again.

"I'll be back first thing—" Tab said in a committed tone.

Isabella interrupted him. "No, *we'll* be back in the morning."

For the first time in hours, Tab felt some relief as his fatigue gripped him hard.

She said to Benjamin, "Don't worry. I'll make sure he gets home safely."

Tab smiled at Isabella. "Don't worry, Grandpa. You've trained her well. I know who the boss is now." It was a surprise he could muster a moment of levity.

She smiled back and hooked her arm around his. "We'll see you in the morning." And she pulled Tab toward the door.

Tab was reluctant to leave, but he knew there was nothing he could do. They walked together toward the elevator, both eager to get some sleep.

Tab was starting to realize he was going to need to rely on others for help. That was something he was as unfamiliar with as he was uncomfortable.

But if he had to rely on someone, he was glad that person was Isabella.

Chapter 12

❧

The Blessing

EXHAUSTED FROM THE NIGHT'S VIGIL, Tab returned from the hospital about the same time he would have been getting up. He laid in bed trying to get the sleep his body so desperately needed, but the events of the previous day kept running through his head like an endless loop.

Tab thought his encounter with the old man seemed so strange. Why did he sit next to him? How did he know what to say? And most importantly, where did Tab put those beads?

Tab struggled to stay in bed even though it was only six in the morning. He was so used to starting his day with the sun; it was part of him now. He decided to get over to the shop and clean up the blood before Isabella saw it.

When he arrived, the bench that had been moved outside was no longer there. He parked his car and ran over to the shop.

He was relieved to find the door locked.

Tab never carried the old skeleton key, and it wasn't in the house the night before, so he would have to find the spare key in his grandmother's desk. As he opened the back door of the house, he noticed it was hanging on the nail right where it should be. His sleep-starved head wasn't making sense of it all. When he entered the shop, it was neat as a pin— not a trace of the horror he saw the night before.

It was a bit of a head scratcher until his grandfather's neighbor knocked on the door.

"Oh. Hi, Mr. Murphy."

"Hello, Tab. We heard what happened. How's your grandfather?"

"They repaired his hip last night. The doctor said he thinks with a lot of hard work and therapy, he'll make a full recovery. I'm going to go and see him in a little bit." His eyes wandered back to the tidy room.

"I hope you don't mind; we came over and put the shop back together and cleaned everything up. We didn't want you to come home and have to clean it yourself."

"In not sure what to say. This whole thing has been a little overwhelming. Thank you. I really appreciate the help."

"You're welcome, Tab. You know, your grandfather is very special to us here in the neighborhood. He has helped all of us at one time or another."

"Well, I really appreciate it. I didn't even know anyone else had a key to the shop."

"Your grandfather gave me keys to his house and shop long before you were even born. We've been neighbors for more than forty years. It has been an honor to know him and call him my friend. If there's anything I can do, please let me know. We want to help."

"I sure will, and I'll tell Grandpa how much help you've been already."

"It's been good to talk to you, Tab, and that offer is for you too. Please don't hesitate to call. I'll let you go. I'm sure you want to get going. See you later."

"Thanks again." Tab waved and watched him walk across the yard.

Even though he knew his grandfather had helped his neighbors over the years, he was seeing for the first time how much he meant to them.

Tab went to his grandfather's desk and took the clipboard that kept all the orders off the wall. He looked through the list and wondered how they were ever going to be filled. Mr. Mendenhall—now that was a project Tab was looking forward to. He had already found the mechanical parts he was going to need for the TV. "Flattened TV," he said as the Kirkman grin he inherited returned. Even though there wasn't a single project on the list he felt he couldn't handle, he felt a little unsure he could continue without his master and muse.

Tab always did his best work for his grandfather because he never wanted to let him down. He wondered if his grandpa would ever be well enough to pick up another tool. He sat on the stool and just stared out the window. Those feelings of being alone started to creep back in.

159

He tossed the clipboard down on the desk and looked around the shop for a moment before he closed the door behind him and locked it with the old skeleton key. He bounced the key in his palm a couple of times and then took his own ring of keys out of his pocket and fed the skeleton key through the keyring.

He made his way to the diner where he was going to meet Isabella before they went to the hospital.

Isabella arrived a little early and sat in their old booth and waved to him as he walked in.

"Excuse me, young lady. Are you alone, or are you waiting for that skinny kid you used to come in with?"

"No, I've traded him in for an older man, but you can sit with me until he gets here."

"Oh, good. I hate to eat alone. I'm sure I'll be done before he gets here," Tab said as he plopped down in the seat across from her.

"How are you doing?" she said as she noticed his demeanor.

"Okay, I think. I can't stop thinking about my grandfather and what he's going through. I'm anxious to get back to see him."

"Then let's eat and head back to the hospital."

Isabella kept their conversation going even after they ordered. Tab tried to listen, but his thoughts were clouded. Although he knew he had support from Isabella, he struggled with how he would balance all the responsibilities of the shop and help with his grandfather's rehab.

"Tab ... Tab?" Isabella looked at him with concern.

"Sorry, my mind wandered."

Isabella gave him a compassionate smile. Then she did something she had only done once before at their senior prom. While they were getting their picture taken, she reached over and took Tab's hand in hers and laced her fingers in his.

Tab looked at her with surprise. He felt reassured as she said, "Last night when we were in the waiting room and I looked over at you sitting by yourself ... I felt this amazing feeling of warmth and peace like I've never felt before. I knew everything was going to be all right. It was so wonderful I had to smile."

She reached across the table and took his other hand. "Tab, we can do this. I want to help."

Tab looked at Isabella and felt a peace come over him. Ever since he made that feeble prayer, he felt an undeniable contentment. His fear of being alone was fading away. He didn't know how or when, but he knew he and Isabella would become more than friends.

He squeezed her hand and said, "Okay … I think we can do it too."

The server arrived with their food and apologized for how long it took. Tab smiled and said, "No, your timing is perfect. Thank you."

They finished their meal, and Tab ordered his grandfather's favorite sandwich to go. Tab was sure it was the only place in all of Connecticut that made goose liver sandwiches.

As they left the diner, Isabella said, "We have to go to Benjamin's house before we go. I want to get something for him."

"What is it?"

"Your grandmother's photo. His day can't end until he says good night to her."

"You're right. It will mean a lot to him that you remembered."

Tab and Isabella entered Benjamin's room, looking very surprised to see him sitting in a chair eating a cup of Jell-O.

He gave them a big grin and said with a hoarse voice, "My two favorite people. Don't look so surprised. You've seen me eat Jell-O before."

Tab grinned back. "I'm not looking at the Jell-O. I can't believe you're not still in bed."

"The nurse said I could get out of bed as soon as I thought I was ready, and I said how about now. So here I am eating some strawberry Jell-O."

"Maybe you'd prefer to eat this." Tab held up a paper bag. "Goose liver and onions on rye."

"I've taught my apprentice well," he said, reaching for the prize.

Isabella squeezed in front of Tab and gave Benjamin a gentle hug. "I have something for you too."

"Oh, my Ellen. How thoughtful of you. I didn't get to see her last night when I said good night."

Tab's phone rang just as Isabella set Ellen's picture on the table next to Benjamin's bed. "It's Uncle Ronny."

"Here's Grandpa … Can you take the phone?" he asked as he reached to hand his grandfather the phone.

Benjamin untangled his hand from his IV and took the phone from Tab. "Hello, Ronny. I got myself in a little trouble."

"Dad! I can't believe it … You sound pretty good!"

"I'm still here."

"It sounds like it! Poor Tab sounded a little flustered when he called."

"That's my Tab. He saved my life last night when he found me. It was nothing short of a miracle. The doctor said I would have surely passed if I had laid there until morning."

"Well, listen, Dad. I called in for emergency leave so I can come and help."

"You know I would love to see you, but you don't need to do that. I've got all the help I need. Tab and Isabella are here to take care of me."

"I'll give you a call when I have my travel plans. I should be there in a day or two."

"I'm looking forward to seeing you, Son."

"Me too. I've got to get going, I'll see you soon … Okay? I love you!"

"I love you too, Ronny … bye-bye."

He looked at the phone, trying to figure out how to hang up. Tab took the phone from him. "Sounds like Uncle Ronny is coming."

"He'll be here in a few days."

"How are you doing?" the nurse said as she walked in the room.

"I think I'm getting a little tired."

"Let's get you back in bed. We don't want you sitting too long for the next few days."

Tab and Isabella stood up, ready to help as Benjamin pulled his walker in front of him. They each supported an arm. Benjamin grimaced as he pulled himself to his feet.

"Oh my!" he said as he steadied himself.

"Are you ready? Remember, small steps," the nurse reminded him.

Benjamin shuffled his feet slowly to get the three feet to his bed. He gripped his walker with all his strength.

Isabella supported his arm. "You're almost there!"

The nurse reminded him not to twist his foot. "Lift your foot; don't twist at the hip," she said as he turned to sit on the bed.

He slowly lowered himself down on the bed and said, "This is the hard part."

The nurse showed Tab and Isabella how to help him lift his leg into bed.

"Make sure not to twist the leg. Keep his toes pointing up."

Benjamin winced as he got settled in. "That will take it out of you."

Exhausted, he laid his head back on his pillow and let out a big exhale. The long recovery he was facing was starting to sink in. The feeling of helplessness was unfamiliar territory.

Another nurse came in to take all his vital signs and checked to make sure his IV was working. She asked what his pain level was, and he responded honestly. "About a seven right now, but I just got back in bed. Before that, it was about a four."

"Push your button now if you need more pain medicine."

Benjamin held up the button that would administer the pain medicine by IV. "It makes me sleepy when I use it."

The nurse said, "Right now it's better for you to be sleepy rather than in pain. Let's set your goal to not letting it get over a five." She walked over to the eraser board and wrote her name. "My name is Sue; I'll be your nurse for the day. If you need anything, ask for me. Let's work on your pain level." She wrote down the number five. "Let's make that your pain goal for today. When you feel it going up, push your button."

Sue reminded Benjamin of an old drill sergeant he had long ago.

She finished checking his vitals. "Call me if you need anything," she said and left the room.

"Is there anything we can do for you?" asked Tab as he noticed his grandfather's eyes beginning to close.

"I'm feeling okay right now, but the medicine will be putting me to sleep in a few minutes. I don't want you spending all day here staring at me. Why don't you come back this evening for a little while." He shifted his pillow and closed his eyes. "I've got all the wonderful nurses taking care of my every need." His voice started to trail off. "I'll be right here when you come back."

The last thing he heard as he drifted off was Isabella's quiet voice. "Let's go and let him get some sleep."

Tab and Isabella came every day to help Benjamin. He worked

hard to make his way up and down the hall before he was released from the hospital.

Tab and Ronny made arrangements for his rehab at a nearby nursing home. It was just ten minutes from the shop, so Tab could visit often. Friends from church made sure he had everything he needed.

Benjamin would need to spend several weeks there before he would be able to climb the steps up to his bedroom.

During one of Tab's visits, a therapist came to check on him. She asked if he was ready to take a few more steps.

Benjamin nodded. "I have my helpers here now. Let's see if I can make it down to the nurse's station and back."

"If you're up for it, let's go."

Benjamin gripped his walker tightly and wrenched himself to his feet. "Okay, let's go."

Tab slowly walked alongside him as he made his way down the hall. The therapist followed behind with a wheelchair, constantly asking how he was doing. By the time he returned to his room, he was exhausted from his effort.

Tab helped him get settled back into his bed.

Benjamin wiped the sweat from his brow. "Whew! That really took it out of me. That's my second time today. Don't you worry. I'll be running a mile or two before you know it."

Tab gave him a pained smile. "I'm sure you will."

Perhaps they both knew it was going to be a while. He wondered himself how he was ever going to return to his life from before his fall. His doctor told him his hip could take up to a year to heal, but his knees were another matter. He knew he had few options. He had to have both knees replaced as soon as his doctor was willing to do them.

Tab did his best to keep his work routine the same, but the shop was a terribly lonely place without his grandfather. He missed his grandfather's watchful and critical eye.

He often struggled to keep his concentration and was grateful when Isabella's schedule allowed her time to hang out at the shop.

With nearly a year's backlog of orders on his grandfather's old clipboard, Tab wondered if he could keep up the pace needed to complete them on time. He even limited his time with his highboy challenge to one day a week.

Every day he gave his grandfather a progress report and even showed him a picture or two on his smartphone.

Tab called Mr. Campbell to let him know what had happened and to assure him that the restoration of the old Tabner highboy was nearly complete.

Mr. Campbell quickly said, "Never mind the old dresser. How's your grandfather doing? Would it be all right if I called him?"

He even asked about Tab and if there was anything he could do for him, which surprised Tab. It still felt a little strange to him that someone as wealthy and important as Mr. Campbell would be concerned about his welfare, but he was pleased he wanted to talk with his grandfather.

"I'm sure Grandpa would love to hear from you." Tab knew the two of them had made an instant connection, both admiring each other's passion for fine furniture. He gave Mr. Campbell the number to the nursing home and thanked him.

The days were quickly growing shorter. Tab supplemented his *Farmer's Almanac* with the forecast on the internet to make sure he was choosing the days with the most sunlight. He wanted to plan out his days, using the clear and sunny days to work on his highboy.

Tab was nearly done with his own highboy; he only had two big things to do before finishing the woodworking: the finials and top drawer with the carved shell design.

The lathe he was going to use to make the finials was outdated when old Tabner used it. Tab felt funny with the thought of having his grandfather spin the six-foot power wheel that turned the lathe. Now, Isabella would have to be his stand in.

It took Tab a while to figure out the right speed and even the right place to stand to grab the wheel to spin it with a smooth and constant speed.

Isabella watched with fascination. Tab fussed over tightening the two-inch-wide leather belt that wrapped around the pulley on the jack shaft above the lathe. Another belt connected the jack shaft to the pulley on the lathe. It took nearly a day for him to make all the adjustments.

When it was Isabella's turn to spin the giant wheel, she needed Tab's help to get it started. Once it got up to speed, she was able to keep it going without much effort.

After making a practice piece to get familiar with the lathe, he was able to make short work of turning the three pieces. All he needed now was to do the carving of the spirals into their tops.

Tab made a place near the window to get just the right light. He wanted to have a strong shadow on his work so he could see the evenness of the spiral grooves he was carving into the finials. It would have been easier to do this with his bench lamp. He could simply move it to whatever position he needed, but the sun was far less cooperative. He found he had to continually move down the length of his bench as the sun made its arc across the sky.

Isabella seemed just as drawn to watching Tab carve as she was his grandfather. Once she even sat on the bench next to him to get a better look at what he was doing.

Isabella's presence in the shop was more than just someone keeping him company. Ever since their year together in high school, there wasn't anyone he felt as comfortable with.

They could talk about anything and everything. He told her about his strange encounter with the old man at the hospital and how something changed when he held those beads in his hand.

Isabella visibly shivered as he recounted his conversation, and she started to smile as he told her about his feeble prayer.

She looked outside at the beautiful fall day. As she stretched, she said, "Tab, I think you need to get away from everything that's been going on. Let's just go for a drive and spend some time together."

Tab always liked to spend time with Isabella, so he quickly agreed. They cleaned the benches and swept the shop as his grandfather always did to prepare it for the next day, but before they could make their escape, the phone rang.

Tab reluctantly answered, hoping he could just take a quick message so they could be on their way. "Hello, Kirkman's." He was pleasantly surprised to hear Mr. Campbell's voice.

"Hello, Tab. How are you?"

"I'm doing well. I've got your highboy ready, and my own is almost complete. I just have to finish carving the finials and do a little adjusting on my drawers."

"That sounds great, Tab. I'm looking forward to seeing it when you're done."

"Thank you. I would be honored."

"I wanted you to know that we had a wonderful visit with your grandfather. He said you've been working hard in his absence. We thought it would be nice to invite you and your girlfriend out to our beach house on Long Island. We have something important to show you. Can you come by tomorrow?"

Tab was already intrigued by the mystery, and he was thrilled to spend another day with Isabella. He didn't hesitate. "I would love to. I'll have to check with Isabella to see if she's free tomorrow." As he glanced her way, she nodded.

"Okay, we'll be there."

Tab wrote down the address and said goodbye.

Isabella said, "So, what's that all about?"

"Mr. Campbell said he wants to show me something."

"What do you think it is?" she said out of extreme curiosity.

"I have no idea, but everything in their other house is fabulous … You're going to love it!"

"It sounds great, but we have an adventure of our own. Let's get going before the phone rings again."

"I'm right behind you."

Tab followed Isabella out the door and locked it with the old skeleton key. In a few minutes, they were in his car. Tab had no idea where to go, so they just headed north. After a while, he saw a sign that said twenty miles to Chicopee. He started to chuckle as he mouthed the word Chicopee.

"What's so funny? Come on, Tab … Tell me," she urged as she started to giggle along with him.

"That sign back there said *Chicopee*. I remember going for a drive with my mom and dad on a Sunday afternoon. I was about six years old, and my mom was having me read the signs along the way. When I saw the sign for Chicopee, I started to laugh. You know how little kids get silly about anything to do with the bathroom. Well, that was the first time I ever saw the word Chicopee, and I couldn't stop laughing. After a few minutes, we were all laughing."

"That's a great memory, Tab. I think that's the first time you've told me a sweet story like that."

Tab got quiet again, his throat tightening at the thought of his parents. "I really miss them, you know. I loved our Sunday trips."

"Can you remember more about that day?"

"Mom would have her notepad with the addresses of antique shops that she wanted to visit. She would pack our lunch in a cooler, and we would eat in the car on the way. The day we went to Chicopee we went to several antique stores, and I remember Mom got so excited that she found an old chair that she thought was a Kirkman. That was the beginning of her passion to collect old Kirkman furniture."

"Hey, Tab, I have an idea … Why don't we go to Chicopee and see if we can find that antique store. Who knows, maybe we can find a Kirkman we can buy."

Tab said, "Okay, let's do it!"

Tab couldn't remember much about the antique store except that it was near a bridge over the river. They drove west along the river on Main Street. Isabella scanned the storefronts for anything that looked like an antique store.

Tab said, "There's the bridge. We must be getting close." He looked for anything that was familiar.

The closer they got, the more he remembered the memory of his mother's voice. "Charles, let's park here, and we'll walk the street." It rang so clearly in his head that he looked at the passenger's seat to see if she was there.

At that moment, Isabella's words echoed similarly from what he'd heard almost twenty years ago.

She pointed and said, "There's something! Find somewhere to park, and we'll walk up the street and take a look."

Tab couldn't help but smile and shake his head as he wheeled his car into a parking spot.

"What is going on with you today?" she asked.

He smiled again with his big Kirkman grin, "This is so weird!"

"What are you talking about?"

"My memory of this place is so vivid. I remember my mom saying almost the exact same thing you just did. I even expected to see my mom when I looked at where you were sitting."

Isabella took Tab by the arm as they walked down the street. "What else do you remember about that day?"

"It was hot, and I remember the car was like an oven when we got back. It was a beautiful clear day like today, but you know summer."

"Anything else?"

"My dad could look through the antique stores in about ten minutes, but my mom would look at everything. She didn't want to miss a thing!" Tab smiled again and said, "My dad would go through the store two or three times. He told my mom that he just wanted to be thorough, but my mom knew he was just being polite and trying not to rush her. When he wanted to push her just a little, he would walk behind her. He unsuspectingly managed to get her to walk a little faster."

Isabella wrapped her arm around Tab's and held it tightly as they walked. Even though it was a bright sunny day, the brisk blustery air sent the season's golden leaves swirling around their feet.

Tab pointed. "Here it is. I'm sure this is the one," he said as he held the door for Isabella.

The musty smell brought back even more memories. He stood near the front counter as the moments of the past clicked by like a home movie. Isabella went ahead exploring the old treasures.

It took a while for Tab to shake off the memories. As he followed Isabella from one booth to another, it slowly occurred to him that these memories didn't hurt anymore. He was so used to his anger and sadness about the loss of his parents invading his memories that he never let himself go there, but today was somehow different.

He felt a little funny about his persistent smile as he followed Isabella into another packed booth.

Isabella pointed out several chairs for him to look at, but none of them had what he knew were the telltale signs that told him it was made by one of his ancestors. Tab had little hope to find a Kirkman chair or anything that his family would have made.

They made their way to the back of the store. Nothing caught his eye until Isabella lifted a stack of old hat boxes off a small stool.

As she handed Tab the boxes, he said, "Stetson … nice!"

She knelt on the floor and lifted the stool to get a closer look. "No, silly. This!"

Tab recognized the shape right away as he knelt down on one knee next to her. She leaned against him. "What do you think? Is it a Kirkman?"

Tab took the stool from her as she lifted it in his direction. The little four-legged stool was a common shape made by many makers over the years. It was without a doubt old, its black paint worn thin and the hard maple underneath stained and polished with years of use.

Tab was looking for anything that would tell him it was made by a member of his family. He thought it looked exactly the same as the stool that his grandfather had fallen from.

As he turned it, he saw something familiar—a small, quarter-inch wooden peg that was in the edge of the seat. He had seen it in many of the chairs that he had made with his grandfather.

When he asked his grandfather why he put them in he said, "Well, it's something I've always done to every chair."

Tab looked up at Isabella and with confidence said, "Grandpa made it. I'm sure of it."

Isabella was delighted. "When I suggested we find a Kirkman chair, I never dreamed we would find something."

Tab showed Isabella the little peg on the edge of the seat. "You see this … Grandpa does this to all his chairs."

"Are you sure?"

"Sure, I'm sure. The chairs I'm working on right now have them. Tab had a big grin on his face. "I can't wait to show it to Grandpa. I'm sure he would love to see one of his old stools."

After they paid, Isabella clutched her prize as they walked back to the car. Tab walked beside her. He was still feeling pretty good, not about the little stool but about the new peace that came from old memories.

He opened the door for her and placed the stool on the seat behind him before getting in himself.

Isabella put her hand on Tab's arm as he placed the key in the ignition. "Tab, can we talk for a minute?"

He sat back in his seat, not sure what she wanted to say, but the day had gone so well that he thought something surely was going to return him to his familiar funk. "Of course. What's on your mind?"

"Tab, I've been a little afraid to talk to you about this."

He felt his whole body start to tingle from the tension of the moment.

"I know you hoped we could continue our friendship just as it was before I left for school." Tab's mind started to fill in the next sentence he expected her to say.

"But, Tab, I just can't do it anymore!"

He recoiled from the words and pulled his hand away. He quickly apologized for whatever he had done to offend her. His words were all a jumble as he tried to reconcile how wonderful the day had gone with what she was saying.

She stopped him midsentence. "Tab!" she exclaimed as she shushed him. "Let me finish." She reached over and placed her hand on his chin. "Look at me … I don't want that anymore … I want you to do something for me."

He looked at her with his eyes ready to flow with tears from his confusion.

"I want you to ask me out on a date … right now! A real date … tonight. And I'm not going to let you start the car until you do." Her own eyes started to tear up as she waited for his reply.

Tab sat motionless, trying to process everything she said. She didn't want to simply be friends anymore. She wanted more. Was he hearing her right? After a few breathless attempts, he uttered a feeble, "Sure."

She smiled with relief and again got serious. "No, Tab, that won't do! You have to say it … I want you to ask me."

Tab sat up in his seat and cleared his voice. "Miss Sabatini, it would be my pleasure to ask you out to dinner tonight."

"*Date!* Tab, say the word."

"Will you go out on a date with me tonight?"

With a blushing smile, she said, "I would love to."

Tab's head was still swimming as Isabella said, "Let's get going. I've got a lot to do."

"A lot to do?"

"Yes, I have to find the right dress and maybe do something with my hair."

"Really? All that for pizza?" Tab seemed a bit confused.

Isabella looked at him a bit cross-eyed. "Pizza?! I don't think so ... and you better be wearing a jacket and tie."

Tab had just been thrown right out of his comfort zone. However, much to his surprise, panic wasn't the emotion he was feeling. If he were going to turn his life upside down, there wasn't anyone else in the world he would rather do it with.

Their drive home was filled with conversation. Isabella had him thinking about going places he would never have considered before. Even the idea of going to Germany to see Willy and Celeste seemed to interest him.

Tab's eyes popped open at the annoying time of five o'clock in the morning. Even though he wasn't going in to work, he just couldn't sleep anymore. Just the thought of picking up Isabella and having breakfast at their favorite booth at the diner before heading off for the Campbell's beach house made him too excited to sleep anymore.

Neither one of them had ever taken the Cross-Sound Ferry to Long Island before, so they thought it would be fun. Crossing in November was gray and cold, but it was not enough to dampen their spirits.

Isabella took full advantage of the chilly morning and insisted Tab put his arms around her to keep her warm.

Yesterday had been filled with lots of firsts. It was the first time he had been on a date with Isabella, the first time since his parents had died that he could think about them without feeling depressed, and the first time he kissed Isabella good night. For the first time in his adult life, he was looking forward to what was coming next.

He was excited to introduce Isabella to the Campbells. He smiled when he thought about the phone call. When Mr. Campbell called, he had referred to Isabella as his girlfriend, and now she was.

They arrived at the Campbell's giant beach house right on time.

Tab told Isabella about the Campbells' incredible house in Rye and the fantastic old treasures they had.

He expected to see more of the same, but when they were invited inside, he was surprised by all the modern furniture and artwork.

Tab introduced Isabella and expressed his surprise to Mr. and Mrs. Campbell about all the modern artwork.

"This is my wife's passion," said Mr. Campbell, glancing fondly at Connie. "She has taught me a lot about the quality of modern artists. It's a real challenge to see potential and pick pieces that work well in the collection. We have all afternoon. Would you like to look around?"

Tab and Isabella eagerly accepted the invitation. The Campbells gave them a tour of the house, pointing out each piece and telling stories about the artists and craftsmen. Mrs. Campbell explained how she found each piece and how they even commissioned several of them.

After their tour of the first floor, Mr. Campbell said, "Now let's go upstairs. We have something we want to show you."

They followed the Campbells up the stairs and down the long hall. Mr. Campbell opened a door and invited them in.

Tab and Isabella walked in … to a completely empty room.

They both looked around a little confused as the Campbells walked in behind them.

Tab turned and said, "I don't understand."

Mr. Campbell said, "We love collecting antiques, but we felt we had a responsibility to encourage and support young, talented artists and craftsmen too. We want you to make all the furniture for this room."

Tab stood there so stunned he was nearly unable to breathe. He could hardly believe what he had just heard.

Isabella wrapped her hand around his, her smile barely seeming to contain her joy.

Tab looked at the Campbells. "Are you sure?"

Mrs. Campbell said, "We have been talking about it ever since Robert came out to visit your shop to see the highboy. We went and visited your grandfather last week and talked to him about offering you the commission. He is so proud of you and what you have accomplished."

"I don't know what to say … I … I'm in shock. Thank you both so much!" He felt light-headed as he looked around the room again. "How many pieces are you thinking?"

173

Mr. Campbell said, "Why don't we go back downstairs, and we can talk about it over some lunch."

The following day, Tab was eager to talk to his grandfather. He still couldn't believe the Campbells' generous offer.

Tab remembered to bring the stool too. He and Isabella walked into his grandfather's room carrying their prize. He was sitting up in bed watching a football game.

He smiled upon seeing them.

"Hi, Grandpa. How ya feelin'?"

"Not too bad! I took a few more steps with crutches this afternoon. It made me pretty tired, but I think I could go a little farther next time. The therapist wants to start working on going up and down the stairs tomorrow."

Isabella gave Benjamin a welcoming kiss on the cheek, pulled out the stool she had been hiding behind her back, and placed it on his lap.

"What do you have there?" Benjamin asked. "One of my old stools?"

"We went to an old antique shop in Chicopee, and we found this. We thought you might have made it," she said, excited about her find.

Tab pointed at the edge of the seat. "See, it has that little peg like you put in all your chairs."

He turned the stool and looked at one side and then the other, "No ... No ... I'm sure *I* didn't make it, but it is a Kirkman that's for sure. I think it's my grandfather's work. He and my father's work are almost impossible to tell apart, especially their chairs and stools."

Isabella had to ask, "So, Benjamin, what's up with the peg?"

"It's an old family tradition. The Kirkmans have always done it. I hope Tab will continue it when he takes over the"—he stopped mid-sentence when Isabella gave Tab a secretive smile—"Isabella, did you want to say something?"

His grandfather looked back and forth between them with his eyebrows raised.

With a silly smirk on his face, Tab said, "We went out on a date last night."

Benjamin looked at her and said with an approving smile, "Really?! A date? Is that true?"

Isabella nodded as she reached to give him a big hug.

"My, my, good for you!"

Something happened that Tab hadn't seen in a long time. Tears filled his grandfather's eyes.

"Come on. What's the big deal? It was just a date."

"Tab, I never thought I'd see this day."

Isabella's phone chirped in her purse with the sound of Chinese music. "It's my mom. I told her I'd tell her about the Campbells' beach house. I better take this outside," she said, excusing herself with a smile.

"Beach house?" Benjamin asked.

Tab told him about the huge beach house filled with all the contemporary art and furniture and how the Campbells showed them the empty room and offered him a commission to build enough furniture for an entire room.

"When they visited me last week and told me what they wanted to do, I was so happy for you that I could barely keep it a secret. I didn't know until now if you were going to continue making furniture. I've always had it in the back of my mind that you wished you had gone into the army with Willy."

"How did you know about that?"

"Your Uncle Ronny was as concerned as I was about what you were going to do after school. We both wanted it to be your choice, so we didn't let on that we had been talking."

"I wanted to, and I felt like I wanted to get as far away from the memories as I could ... but I couldn't ... I made a promise."

"What promise?"

Tab shook his head. "I couldn't go. That day when Mom waited for me to give her a hug, she said, 'Promise me you'll take good care of your grandfather.' I didn't say anything back to her as I pulled away, but as they drove away, I yelled to her "I—""

"I promise," his grandfather finished. "I remember."

"It was the last thing I ever said to them. You see ... I couldn't go. I had to keep my promise."

His grandfather's eyes teared up again. "My little apprentice," he said in a quivering voice. "I didn't know ... I'm so sorry you've carried that burden for so long." He wiped his eyes and took a deep breath. "Tab,

I know how unhappy you have been ever since your parents died … how that awful day stole the joy from your life. I hoped that somehow, some day, you could let go of your anger and find happiness and contentment."

Tab felt a flood of emotions racing through his veins. Ever since that fateful day, he lived every day with fear that he would forever be alone. He tried to respond, but the emotions kept the words from coming.

Finally, he said, "That day that you fell in the shop and I found you on the floor … It brought back all those feelings that I had the day Mom and Dad died. All I could think about was how I was going to lose you too. I felt like I was going to be all alone, but something happened that day." He looked into his grandfather's eyes. "I did something I hadn't done in nine years … I saw Isabella crying, and I decided to pray that she could be happy. It was just a short prayer. I hoped my prayer would change her … but instead … it changed … me," he said as he thumped his chest with his voice quivering.

"Tab … my little apprentice … don't you know … When you bless others, God blesses you! God pricked your heart when you reached out for Isabella with your prayer. You thought he had abandoned you, but he was always with you. All you needed to do was reach out to him."

Tab placed his head in his hands. "These last few weeks have been filled with so many highs and lows that it's been really hard to handle it all."

"Tab, that's what life is. Somehow, we have to learn how to celebrate the good and survive the bad. Both of us have suffered horrible losses, but we got through the bad times. Now it's time for you to find the joy that's been missing in your life. Let Isabella show you the way."

"Hey! What's going on here?"

Tab turned to see Isabella standing in the doorway with a puzzled expression on her face.

Benjamin quickly said, "Oh, I'm so happy for the two of you. I'm feeling a little emotional about it. Come over here and give me another hug."

Tab was relieved his grandfather deflected the attention off him. He did his best to wipe away his tears before Isabella could see he had been crying too.

"Okay, you two, I think I've had all the excitement I can handle for one day. It's been a big day. You two go home and let me get some rest."

They said their goodbyes, and as they walked out the door, they tried to decide what to do next.

Tab was anxious to get started the next morning. He had finished carving the finials early in the morning, leaving the last piece of his highboy to complete—the top drawer with the carved shell. He made the little hidden drawer and the carved drawer to the same exact measurements as on old Tabner's drawings. Throughout the challenge and everything that had happened, he stayed true to his grandfather's wishes and stopped working every day with the setting sun.

Today, he was ready to do a final fit.

He wanted to finish his work on the highboy today so he could bring his grandfather over for his first visit to the shop since his fall. He wanted to get his approval before he started the long process of applying the finish.

The only tool he needed was a block plane to shave off a little bit here and there to make the drawer fit perfectly.

This was a big moment for Tab. His work on the highboy had to be precise so that everything would look crisp and the space around each drawer was exactly the same on all sides and equal to each other.

He took his grandfather's old stool and set it in front of the highboy. The little inner drawer and the fancy fan-carved drawer were placed on the bench within easy reach.

He held the little drawer up to the opening and then carefully pushed it into place. He could tell it was a snug fit, but he wanted to make sure it wouldn't get too tight when the humidity was high. He slowly pulled it back out. As he did, he could hear the suction of air created by its tight fit. After a few swipes of his plane on each side, he slid it back in for another fit.

This time it was nearly perfect. He pushed it in and pulled it out repeatedly, trying to get a feel for how it fit. Then the final drawer was to be fit. He carefully lifted it off the bench and tipped it into its opening.

This was a proud moment. The complete vision was coming into view as he inched the drawer into its opening with his fingertips.

He could feel the hair on his head flutter as the air was displaced by the drawer. He smiled as it was nearly into its final place. His smile quickly disappeared as the drawer front kept going in until it was a full half inch past its intended place.

His face felt hot at the realization of his failure. He stood there for a moment, trying to keep his composure.

Without saying a word, he stepped down from the stool and sat at old Tabner's drawing bench with his highboy at his back. He knew he had checked the measurements over and over. He had even measured the original on old Tabner's highboy. This was a stupid mistake and a big one.

"Time to go see Grandpa," he said out loud to himself.

Tab arrived just in time to head down to physical therapy with him.

By the end of the hour, Tab could tell he was tired as the sweat soaked his shirt. There was no doubt he was working hard every day to get out of the nursing home as soon as possible.

Tab walked alongside him as he slowly made his way back to his room. His grandfather leaned his crutches against the wall and held the railing of the bed for the last two steps.

"Oh my! That really takes it out of me. I take one of my pain pills just before I go down to therapy so I don't hurt as much when I get back to my room, but they make me so groggy. I can see why they don't want you to use heavy machinery while taking them," he said with a grin.

Tab took his water bottle and put fresh water in it while his grandfather got settled into bed. "I'm glad to see you're working so hard at therapy. I need you back in the shop. It was a pretty disappointing morning."

"What's going on?"

"I just made a mistake on the highboy, that's all." Tab was so disappointed with himself that he couldn't make eye contact.

"Tell me what's wrong."

"Well, it's no big deal. I had everything finished on the highboy. All I had to do was finish fitting the top two drawers. I was so happy with myself as I pushed the fan-carved drawer into its recess, but it kept going right past flush. I can't believe I screwed up so badly." Tab's eyes were still fixed on the floor, unwilling to look up at his grandfather.

When he looked up, his grandfather's eyes were closed and he spoke in a groggy voice. "It'll fit fine. You won't need to make a new drawer. Don't forget the blessing. You'll need your toy now that you're the elder craftsman ..." and he drifted off to sleep.

Tab sat there confused by his grandfather's sleepy comments. Wasn't he the elder craftsman? Tab was sure he could never fill his grandfather's shoes. You'll need your toy? And the blessing?

He drew the blankets up around his grandfather and let him sleep.

He returned to the shop and tried to figure out why the drawer was too short. He put the little drawer in first and then the carved shell, and they went in almost a half inch too far.

He looked at the drawings of old Tabner's piece again, and his measurements were right. He decided to try the new drawers in the old dresser, and they fit perfectly.

Nothing was making sense, especially what his grandfather said about how the drawer should fit.

Tab was sitting in a chair in the middle of the shop just looking at the highboy when Isabella stopped by. He barely acknowledged her presence as she entered the room.

"Hey, what's going on here?" She stroked her hand across Tab's shoulder.

"I made a mistake somehow. The top drawer is a half inch too short."

"That doesn't sound so bad. Can't you just put something behind it or something?"

Tab looked up at her as he shook his head. "No ... not on this thing. It won't be perfect ... and I'll know it."

"Okay, then how do you fix it?"

"Well, according to Grandpa, it is perfect and will fit, and I can't for the life of me figure out what he meant."

"What did he say?"

"Well, he had just finished his therapy and was drifting off to sleep, so it was hard to understand. He said four things." He held up his fingers as he counted them out. "It'll fit, don't forget the blessing, I'll need my toy, and I'm the senior craftsman now."

"So, what do you think all that means?"

With his eyes fixed on the floor, he said, "I've spent all afternoon sitting here trying to figure it out."

Isabella asked, "What do you think the toy is?"

Tab had lots of toys, but maybe his grandfather wasn't talking about a toy at all but a *tool*. The only one he could remember was a little auger drill that he would play with in the shop when he was little.

He told Isabella about the old gimlet and how it threaded like a screw. It had a cutter that would drill a one-eighth-inch hole.

"I would sit and drill hole after hole with it when I was little."

Tab grabbed the drawers again and put them back in the old dresser; they fit exactly. He pulled them back out again and stood on the stool to see if he could feel if there was something that was stopping them from going in too far, but there was nothing.

He grabbed a flashlight to get a better look. Still nothing—nothing but a tiny little hole in the middle of an *X* drawn on the back. It wasn't making any sense.

Then it dawned on him. The little hole in the middle of the *X* was made by his toy.

He looked on the tool rack of his grandfather's bench for the old gimlet. As he reached out to pick it up, he noticed a piece of wood the same size as what was in old Tabner's dresser laying on his grandfather's bench with an *X* and a little hole. He took the gimlet and threaded it into the hole in the back on the old dresser and gave it a tug. To his surprise, the back of the opening came loose. He pulled it out and set it aside.

Grabbing his flashlight again, he shined it into the hole and saw a folded piece of paper.

Tab reached in and pulled it out. The old, thick piece of paper crackled as it resisted Tab's effort to carefully tease it open.

"Wow, this is so cool!" he gasped as he stepped off the stool and sat down next to Isabella to unfold the paper.

As Tab read it carefully, Isabella reached her hand around his shoulders and held him in a warm embrace.

Today is a special day for me. For the first time as senior craftsman, it is my honor to write the blessing and hide it in the dresser. My father and grandfather before him said it was their favorite part of furniture making. They knew that the dresser or table would be useful, but they wanted it to be a blessing. So, I will honor them with this blessing.

O God, take the fruits of these humble hands and let it be a source of joy for all who use it. When they admire it, turn their thoughts instead to the ones they love. As the years go by with every scratch, chip, and worn bit of varnish, may it retain its usefulness and charm.

God, please bless the boys in the shop. Keep them strong and free from sickness. Make their work seem light and fill them with joy, and let their sons and grandsons enjoy the work of their fathers.

Amen,
Tabner Kirkman

CPSIA information can be obtained
at www.ICGtesting.com
Printed in the USA
BVHW031132121120
593127BV00001B/2